Ride with Danger

This is a work of fiction. Any resemblance to places, events, or real people is entirely coincidental.

Written by Kat Blak

Edited by Emma Luna at Moonlight Editing

Formatted by Kat Blak

Front Cover Art by EVE Graphic Design LLC

Dedication

My mum, who had the unfortunate experience of sitting with me in the waiting room waiting to go into court for a speeding ticket. I love you mum, you have pushed me to do my best, even when others said I couldn't do it. You stood by my side though all my crazy and you're still standing by my side as I get crazier. Love you x

From Gabbie Ash: Love you Chola Momma Posh. Thank you for birthing my co-wife and not judging my Mexican ass. I promise to remove the couch from the front garden before you arrive!! And the chickens...maybe.

Blub: Dealing with Traffic Court for a ticket that wasn't even my fault shouldn't have had such an impact. As soon as my eyes snagged on the dark, brooding stranger I had to know him. Talk to him. A compulsion, almost, to make him smile. I don't expect to see him again until suddenly there he is saving me. From life and even myself.

Hope he's ready for one hell of a ride with danger.

Contents

Chapter 1

Chapter One

Isabella

God! I screamed internally. I can't believe that my mother has made me do this. Usually, she wouldn't care and would pass it off to one of our many exclusive lawyers. But since I had scoffed at her suggestion that I become like her, a WASP who spends all of my time at tea parties and raising money for charities that I don't really give a toss about. The only reason she does it is for the tax write off, not for the charities that need the money. Hell, I have told her frequently that the designer clothes she wears to these parties could feed millions of children, and she would just stand there in her Gucci dress and Louboutin shoes and purse her lips at me, making it look like she has an arsehole on her face!

No, I hate that idea, I want to go to Oxford and work as a cognitive neuroscientist. I want to help people with different conditions, help manage them and give them a healthy normal life to live. But according to my stuck up mother, things like that are beneath our family. If I could find other ways of helping people without medicating them, then the pharmaceutical companies would take a big fiscal hit, including my family. Yep, I'm from a family that makes millions of pounds from other people's downfalls. It's why I never tell people my family name, or they would know who I am straight away.

I shift again on the nasty plastic chairs they have us sitting on while we are waiting for our time to head inside and receive my punishment. Whenever I move the horrendous yellow chair makes a squeaking sound that fills the quiet, drab room. All twenty pairs of eyes spin around to look at me directly. I have never enjoyed being the centre of attention, especially in a place like this. I shrink down into my chair with hunched shoulders, hopefully now closing myself off from the world around me. A poke in my ribs causes me to sit straight back up in my chair and turn my death stare onto the young lawyer sitting next to me.

"If your mother caught you sitting slumped over like that she would throw a hissy fit and my hung-over brain couldn't deal with that right now," said Remington III, the young lawyer sitting in the chair next to me. I glance over at him, even sitting down he looks tall, but slim. He has short brown hair with a slight curl and clear bluebell blue eyes. The one thing I have always envied him for is his long dense eyelashes. I always wondered if he was a camel in his past life. Unlike me, who you can often find in sweatpants and a hoodie, he always looks professional and smart. Plus, he always manages to own whatever room he was in, with his personality and dress sense. I look like a natural in a place like this, but he stands out like a sore thumb. Like he is ready to argue his point in a televised murder trail.

"If you think you would ever see my mother in a place like this, you don't know her," I say back to him with a smirk on my lips. I do kinda feel bad for Remi. He is our next-door neighbours' son who has just taken a job at his dad's law firm and now has been sent to baby-sit me. Everyone considers me a wild card, but that's only because I love to piss off my parents and made it my life's mission to annoy the shit out of them. It's my pay-back to them for being fucktards of parents.

"I take it you got your welcome committee last night?" I enquire while looking into his bluebell

9

blue eyes.

"Yes," he responds while trying to read his newspaper. I had heard that when you become an employee at Barron and Carter Law firm they take you to the local strip club and get you blind drunk in the hopes you do something naughty and they can forever hold it over your head! Remi isn't a big drinker, we have been friends for so long and I can count on one hand how many times he has been drunk. He has always been the one to pull my arse out of the fire.

Remi and I are so different and yet still best friends. We were raised completely differently, he was lucky enough to be raised with parents that love him. Even though both his parents have big careers they still take the time to hug and kiss him. They make sure at least once a week to sit down for a family meal; they care and appreciate their son. When he was a kid, they even took time out to do mundane things like homework. In simple terms, his parents had wanted him. Whereas, I was a mistake, one that my mother has never let me forget! A mistake she has held over my head my whole life.

"Issy, you need to stop doing this. You are pretty and intelligent," Remi says with a sigh, down casting his eyes with a slight blush creeping over his cheeks. "Just leave here, leave these arseholes and their bullshit behind and start your life anew."

I look over at him, he would make a good husband one day, loyal to the bone with a huge heart. Our parents have been trying to push us together for years. "We both know that will never happen." I sigh, knowing my life is already over before it has even started. Reaching down into my handbag to grab my AirPods, I slip them into my ears and let the heavy beat and loud vocals of Def Leppard - Pour Some Sugar On Me, wash over me. If I want to get through today, I need to drown my eardrums in some classic rock.

The magistrate court system is first come, first served, and I had slept through my alarms. Yes plural, I need several to get my arse out of bed. I'm easily the furthest away that you can get from being a morning person. In fact, I'm 100% nocturnal. I detest mornings as much as I detest my mother, which really does say a lot. As I was the last one to arrive my case would be the last one to be heard. I may as well get settled for the long haul. Deciding that music is not going to stop the wheels in my brain from turning, I know that reading is always better at stopping my unwanted thoughts, so I get out my iPad. I switch off the music and load up the kindle app; I am 43% of the way through Unveiled by MJ Marstens. It's about a woman who is kidnapped and sold into slavery. It's not my normal read of hot sexy shifters who have a lot of sex, but it's definitely more gripping.

My thoughts start to wander before I can even start reading to block them out. Gazing into the distance, I wonder how different my life could have been. Maybe if I'd been born into a different family, a different life. From the outside my life looks like rainbows and daisies, but from the inside its all demons and darkness.

A clashing sound breaks through my thoughts and brings me back to the present. My flinching at the noise causes Remi to raise his eyebrow at me, if only he knew the demons that haunt me. Like everyone else he only sees an outgoing extrovert, nobody really sees me.

Glancing over my shoulder to see where the noise has come from, I see a boy coming through the metal detectors with worn, ripped jeans and a leather jacket. He seems to be causing a commotion at the security guards desk. They don't waste actual police officers at a place like this, instead we get rent-a-cops who think they're the law. Me and rent-a-cops have crossed paths a time or two over the years. I've made it my mission to make sure they know they're no better than me, and what they say isn't the law. Just because they have this uniform on it makes them think they are above the law and are in command of it. Well, I have news for them, they well and truly don't.

My tutor in secondary school allowed me to take psychology even though my parents said I couldn't. The school just made sure it wasn't on any of my reports sent home, so my parents didn't know. One study we looked at is a famous one in psychology called Stanford Prison Experiment by a researcher called Zimbardo. He wanted to look at the power roles within a prison setting. He created a prison using old lecture halls in the basement of the psychology building. They had the twenty four participants, each assigned to a role of either a prisoner or an officer. The twelve "officers" were given clothes that matched a real prison officer's clothing and a wooden baton. The twelve "prisoners" wore ill fitting, uncomfortable smocks and stocking caps, with chains around one ankle. The researchers found that each man fell into their assigned role quickly. The guards were more prone to punishing the prisoners just because of the setting, roles and the clothes they were in. Which means, you get a fat guy in a rent-a-cop uniform, and their head becomes too big for their bodies and they act like they are better than the rest of society. I want to make sure that they know that's not the case.

A tap on my shoulder brings me back to the present. I must have still been staring toward the metal detectors. I remove one of my earbuds and glance over at Remi who is waiting for my attention.

"What's up?" I say keeping my ear bud in my hand, ready to put it back in my ear. The drone of the vending machines and the beeping of the metal detectors are putting me on edge. I feel better when all the background noise is blocked by the earbuds, even if I'm not playing my music I keep them in.

"You need to fill out one of these forms and have it ready for when we enter the court. Please God don't speak, I'm your representative and I will speak on your behalf." I could tell he is being deadly serious, but telling me not to speak is like waving a red flag at a bull. I'm no feminist but I don't now, nor will I ever need a man to speak for me. Hell, I don't even need a woman to speak for me. I'm rather capable of speaking for myself. You would think after knowing me for most of my life he would know that by now. He obviously saw the flash of anger in my eyes and he let out a huge groan.

"I MEAN it Issy! Please, this is my domain. I know you don't need anyone to talk for you or even on your behalf, but I'm begging. Please just let me talk for you, just this one time. My parents and yours will skin my arse if this doesn't go our way." He looks directly into my eyes, pleading with me to listen to him just this one time.

'Ok," I said, I have seen him looking serious quite often, but nothing like this. I let out a sigh, I'm getting to the end of my patience sitting in this room. I glance around and spot different people also waiting for their time in court. But Remi and I stick out like sore thumbs. Everyone else is dressed in normal clothes; from builders in jeans, to a mechanic dressed in his greasy overalls. Remi however, is sat in a smart Armani suit and tie with shoes so polished I'm sure I could use them as a mirror. Then there's me, wearing a pencil skirt with a smart white shirt. I look like a normal person sitting in an office right now, not a court waiting room. However, mother dearest had gracefully left clothes out ready for me, or at least instructed the maid as to which clothes to give me. Heaven forbid I pick out my own clothes to wear to court. Mother probably thought I would end up wearing a black bag just to piss her off and ruin her life even more.

While looking around the room my eyes land on another set, looking directly at me. I quickly snatch my eyes away from the strangers, as a red blush creeps up my face from embarrassment. Realising he was also staring straight at me and that I shouldn't be embarrassed about it, I slowly moved my eyes back towards him. Yep, he is still looking my way. Nope, I won't be looking away again. Game on, sexy eye man. He has the darkest eyes I have ever seen, like the colour of wet slate. I'm so focused on his eyes, I can't see anything else. This time he is the one to break eye contact first. Yes, I won. I watch as he lowers his eyes to the floor and runs his hands through the longer bits of hair on his head. My gaze follows his hand and I see that his hair is short on the side while being longer on top. His hair is as dark as night, and so glossy. To be honest, I'm jealous of his well-conditioned hair.

He then runs his hand over the short stubble on his chin and across his cheek. Leaving his hand over his mouth, I think I saw a small smirk raising the sides of his lips up, but I can't be sure. I feel a smile adorn my own lips in response and then a less welcomed small poke in my ribs. Turning towards Remi, I ask in a snarky voice, "What?"

"Why are you grinning, you understand what could happen right?" he responds to my question in a pissed off manner.

"I'm not stupid, of course I do!" I snap back, I hate it when people question my level of intellect.

"Then stop grinning like a cheshire cat, and look more remorseful," he snaps back at me.

I turn my eyes back toward the wall in front of me and meet the stranger's eyes again. His eyebrows are pulled down and he wears a frown now. No, I want the smile back, it was like a ray of sunlight in my dark world. No one smiles at me like that. People who know me either smile because they want something, smile with pity, or smile for fakeness. He has a genuinely happy smile that I want to see again. In fact, I would pay good money to see it again. I want to hear his voice too, I bet it's deep and husky.

Glancing over to him, I decide I have to get that smile back. "My doctor told me I have a Vitamin D deficiency. Wanna go back to my place and save me?" I say with my sexiest voice. I hear choking coming from my left and can see Remi looks like he's about to have a heart attack, using his fist to smack on his chest. Looking back over at the stranger, I see that my pick up line didn't even cause him to crack a smile. Fine, I'll have to try again. "My body has 206 bones, want to give me another one?" I don't know how I manage to say it with such a straight face, but I pull it off with only a little smile at the end. I hear some laughter from behind me but ignore it. If I acknowledge the other people they may try to talk to me, not that I mind, I just have someone else in mind to talk to. Ok last try, if this doesn't make him laugh I give up. "I can see that you're busy today, but can you add me to your to-do list?" He raises his hand to cover his mouth and to hide the laugh that I can see bubbling to come out. Yes! I did it. I got that smile back.

"Will you stop? We are not here for you to have fun, this is serious. Do you at least understand that?" Remi snaps at me. Wow, who pissed in his cornflakes this morning? Maybe he is a bran flakes kind of person, bland and tasteless. He used to be fun when we were kids, but his drive to achieve tore that away from him.

"Isabella Jonson," a loud man dressed in a black, loose gown says. He must be the usher. I stand up and take a deep breath, well here goes. Smiling down at the stranger, I decided one last chat up line is worth the hassle Remi will give me. "Do you like to eat mexican, because you're heating up my taco," I joke, but just keep on moving. As I walk down the hall to the courtroom, everyone in the waiting room erupts into laughter, including the stranger.

The fact I'm going in this soon, when I was the last person to check in, means someone paid the rent-a-cop to move my name up the list. I didn't see Remi move from his chair, so his dad or my mother must have, both of which are likely suspects. Down the corridor I see the usher waiting while holding the door open for me. I glance next to me when Remi grabs my arm, stopping me from walking any further. I look up at him, with a mischievous smile on my face.

"Let me do all the talking in there, okay? This is my job, It's what I'm here to do. Just give me this, okay Issy?" he pleads with me. One quick nod back at him has us walking again. All I can hear in my head right now is Darth Vader's theme, The Imperial March.

Chapter Two

Isabella

Walking into the courtroom, I can see straight away the place is designed to intimidate you. Oh how it doesn't work on me. The usher leads me to the defendants stand, where I sit down straight away, and Remi sits just off to the side of me. Already he has his laptop out in front of him with the case file already open. He looks back towards me with a tip of his head and a small smile on his face. This room is one of the only places I see Remi's walls come down and his fighting persona comes out to play.

He stands tall and wide in his smart suit, I guess he is waiting for the judges to arrive. As the door out the back opens up, two judges walk in and take their seats at the table that sits high above everyone else, like they enjoy looking down their noses at everyone. Damn, my mother should have a chair up there with the stuck up judges that are now taking their seats. Behind them also walks a slightly younger blonde lady in a smart suit with minimal makeup on. I would place her in her mid-to-late twenties. She looks over at Remi and smiles. Oh, looks like the lady has a crush on Remi, wonder if he knows. She takes the seat lower down than the judges, but still above the lawyers and convicts. She must be the note taker. I take a slow look around the room. It's big with high ceilings, the wood paneling and green wallpaper is what catches my attention. Plus, the artwork around the room, with its thick gold frames, makes it look gaudy. I would hate to sit in this room all day, it's damn ugly.

"Please stand and confirm your name," the female judge says, staring straight at me. I slowly rise to my feet, taking my time as I'm in no rush. I look her dead in the eyes with a small smile on my face, but not enough to come across bitchy, as I do tend to have a resting bitch face.

"Isabella Jonson, Ma'am," I say strong, but not very loud. I don't want to come across as shouting.

These people have my future in their hands and if they deem me unworthy, I'm fucked. Oh don't get me wrong I would love to see the look on my mother's face and the steam that would no doubt come out of her ears, but poor Remi would be on the end of her wrath too.

"And your age, miss?" she responds back to me, while looking down at the paperwork in front of her. It looks like a big folder that she has in front of her. I would love to see what is written in there about me. I bet everyone of my transgressions is in that file; from streaking naked down the road, to every speeding ticket I have ever gotten. I can't believe I'm sitting in court with the thought of stealing my own file flitting through my mind.

"Twenty, I was born on the eighth of August 1999," I responded quickly, wanting this to be over already. I just want out of this room, out of this place. Hell, I want out of this country and out of my life. I take my seat again, I want Remi to look at me and give me a reassuring smile, but I guess I'm not telepathic as he never glances back.

"This is quite the file you have here, isn't it?" the gentleman glares at me as he asks the question. It looks like he is looking down his nose at me. If there is one thing I can't stand in my life, it's a condescending fucker. People who think they are better than me. It's not like I think highly of myself, but I also know that doesn't make him better than me. Just because he is a lawyer acting as a judge.

"Yes it is." I'm starting to think he's going to make an example out of me with this court proceeding. I slump back in my seat, hating the idea of my life being in this sleazy man's hands.

"Your honour, I would like to remind the court that we are here for the current issue, and not any priors." Remi stands while speaking loud and clear. I want to stand up and give him a 'Whoop Whoop', but that would probably land me in more shit than the mess I'm already in.

The courtroom door creaks open and I glance over at the public viewing area to see who has come in. Tremors run through my body, crap maybe I was wrong. Maybe this time my mother would lower herself to see the downfall of her only daughter. Well that would be a first, maybe the judges would go easier on me with her here, but that's not what I want. I just want to be treated like a normal person. I promise I have no silver spoon up my arse. But instead of my mother, the stranger from the waiting area walks in and sits down.

Huh, that's weird. I look over at his slate grey eyes, which seem to keep my attention anchored on to him. I feel lost just looking into them, almost like they're pools of endless depths. A slight cough brings me back to the present. That was strange, it was like time dropped away from me. Another cough makes me snap my attention back over to the judges, it would seem they have asked me a question and are waiting for my response. Crap, what was the question?

A quick glance over at the gorgeous stranger shows he has a cheeky grin on his face and knew exactly what he had just done. I glance over at Remi in a panic hoping he can help, but his expression is blank and unreadable. Oh screw you all. "Can you repeat the question please?"

With a humph the male judge looks over at me. "Do you plead guilty?"

"Yes," I say, "well no," I carry on in a rush. "Yes and no, is my final answer." I sound like I'm on a game show. Crap, they are not going to like that answer. I can tell by Remi rubbing his temples and the slight shaking of the other lawyer's head that I may have just committed another crime in court. Fuck, I'm all out of luck and feeling flustered as hell.

"Well which one is it?" the lady judge asks me, looking like she may be also losing her patience with me.

"I'm guilty of speeding, but I sent my driving licence off for the points and paid the fine," I say releasing the breath I have been holding. Anyone would think with the way I'm being treated that I killed an animal or a person. Nope, just a speeding ticket left sitting on a side table, which went past the cut-off for a speed awareness course. I think mother did it to punish me, knowing full well I would end up sitting here in this position. It is definitely something she would do. Like the time she left my acceptance letter to Oxford in the fire. So when the butler lit the fire it went up in a plume of smoke. Which I only found out a few weeks ago when I confronted her about it. You would not believe how pissed I was when I found out. Those letters are time limited and mine had passed, so my spot had been given to someone else. Yep, you guessed it, I got in my car and drove away as fast as I could, resulting in another speeding ticket. I think my mother called the police and told them where I was heading just to catch me.

A slight prickling sensation runs down my spine and brings me back to the present. Glancing over, I see the strange man smiling at me. I bet he is smiling because he has found out I'm not a hardened criminal and just a speed demon instead. However, with all my previous transgressions stacked against me, this may not go in my favour. Glancing down at my watch, I see we've been here for ten minutes. Damn, it feels like a whole day has passed.

"Sorry Miss Jonson, do you have somewhere else to be? Are we taking up too much of your time?" I glance up at the male judge, with a shocked look on my face. All I did was look at my watch. I just know deep down he is going to throw the book at me, metaphorically speaking. I wonder who pissed in his corn flakes today. Remi stands up and talks on my behalf, so I zone out.

While I'm daydreaming about the next Ivy Asher book to grace my kindle, I see both judges flash me a look before standing and leaving through the same door they came in through. Fuck are we finished? I don't even know what I've been sentenced to. Damn gargoyle shifter book had me fantasising about being wrapped around several men, getting my freak on and caused me to miss the end of the trial. Glancing over at Remington, I can see he knows I have no idea what my punishment is. He looks two parts embarrassed, and one part pissed. I just don't know if he is pissed at me or the system. I did as he asked, I stayed quiet and kept my mouth shut.

"You got 100 hours of community service," Remi says to me, letting out a long sigh. "It's better than going to prison and with your file, you're lucky that's all you got." Glancing around he spots the stranger still sitting in the viewing area. Keeping his eyes locked on the guy he carries on speaking but in a more whispered tone, "You are now the poster child for all the wealthy kids. No matter how much money your family has, you will still be punished for your crimes. You need to stop messing around and grow the fuck up, as next time they will send you to prison."

I spluttered at his response. "It was only a speed-ing ticket, I can't go to jail for that," I shout and feel my boobs rise up when I cross my arms under them. It's my defence mechanism.

"Issy, you were doing 100 mph over the speed limit. You could have lost your licence for that. To be honest, I think with your history, you got off lightly. As it stands, you have community service, six points on your licence and a fine."

Fuck me side ways, I'm destroying my own life just to get back at my parents. I need to complete this community service and get the hell out of dodge, or I really won't have a future.

Chapter Three

Ryker

Beep Beep Beep. Shitballs, what the hell is on me that's causing this stupid metal detector to go off for the third time? I'm already hating this day and it isn't even mid-morning. Trying to find a fucking court house in the middle of this town was a nightmare. I went into the police station this morning and asked where to find it and they sent me in completely the wrong direction. Then I asked a bus driver, but his accent was so strong that I only managed to understand about four words; left, right, boots, ramp. At the time I had no idea what the guy meant, but I didn't want to ask anymore questions in case he only confused me further. It was only after the first two directions were successful, did I understand what the bus driver had meant by Boots. It's a shop. I have only been in this country a few months now, after being sent over here when my dad died and I had no living relatives left, other than my prostitute mother.

So here I am, living in London with my hooker mother and three siblings whom I knew nothing about. After being raised in America for most of my life, it was a hell of a culture shock. I can't understand why people over here seem to call me 'septic tank', though I don't really care enough to ask why either. I'd had a good life with my dad, only for it all to come crashing down around me. I just have to deal with it for a year and then I can get my life back on track.

After finally getting through security with a huge crash and being eyeballed by the rent-a-cop, who I knew wasn't real police as I'd seen enough of them around the area I was now living in, I took a look around the waiting area and found some empty seats to sit my ass in till my name is called. I kept my eyes downcasted on the floor, I don't want to make eye contact in here and have someone start something. I have been in enough fights since my ass landed in this country, for no other reason than how I look. Apparently, the more badass you look, the more people want to fight with you, but I'm not changing how I look just to suit others. I have always managed to hold my own and I will carry on. So what if I get a few bruised knuckles along the way.

I lounge back in the chair with one ankle resting on my opposite knee and take a casual look around. I can see that the building is old as fuck, with nasty ass stains on the walls and a whole hoard of different people. My eyes land on the girl sitting opposite me who has pastel pink hair that cascades down her back like a waterfall. She is whispering loudly to the smartly dressed man next to her. I don't want to eavesdrop on their conversation, but she has captured my attention. What is someone like her doing in a place like this? It feels strange really, sitting around with all these people who could be on their way to jail. She looks so out of place it's laughable. She looks so innocent. I'm sure when she stands up that sunbeams and rainbows will shoot out of her ass. An ass I would gladly jump.

While daydreaming about having her ass in my hands, I feel the hairs on the back of my neck stand up, bringing me back to the present. Fuck, she is staring right at me. Busted! She has a slight smirk on her face, like she knows what I was thinking about. But fuck me side ways, it's her eyes now that have my attention. They pull me in like magnets, the bottle green orbs are mesmerizing. I raise a hand over my mouth to make sure I'm covering any drool that might be there. I can feel my dick getting hard in my pants and shift slightly in my seat. Fuck, I don't need this right now, not in this room anyway. I force my eyes away from hers and back down to the checkered floor. Running my hand through my longish hair, well longer than it has ever been, I try and think about something else. I need to get the blood away from my dick and back into my brain, if I want to survive today that is. No thoughts seem to help right now, her smile and eyes are branded into my brain, like a cattle mark. I raise my hand to my mouth again to cover the smirk I know is resting on my lips. I take the risk and look back up, and see she is also smirking.

The smart dressed man sat next to her leans over and whispers something into her ear. If this is her boyfriend, I'd imagine he would be pissed about her smirking at another guy so openly. Whatever he's just said to her has royally pissed her off. She snaps something back at him with an angry look maring her beautiful face. I wonder what he could have said to bring such a response out of her. I guess girls don't like being reprimanded by their boyfriends in public. I can feel myself frowning when she brings her eyes back towards me. There seems to now be a big grin on her face.

"My doctor told me I have a Vitamin D deficiency. Wanna go back to my place and save me?" She says in a husky voice. Fuck me, my dick springs back to attention and the choking sounds next to her make my eyes go to the stranger by her side. I see him hitting his chest like he is trying to jump start his heart again. Maybe someone should get him some help. I cant believe his girlfriend has just used a pick up line on me right in front of him. Like, hot damn, the girl has balls.

"My body has 206 bones, want to give me another one?" She asks again with a little smile, but not in the husky voice she used before. Damn, is she trying to start a fight between her and her boyfriend. I'm surprised he hasn't clamped a hand over her mouth and taken her ass out of here. I would have if she was my girlfriend. I would have dragged her ass to the toilet, caveman style, put her over my knees and given her the spanking she obviously needs.

I'm still thinking about giving her a naughty little spanking when I hear her say, "I can see that you're busy today, but can you add me to your to-do list?" Oh God, that is the cheesiest pick up line I have ever heard. I can't help it, I feel my lips turn up into a smile. I raise my hand to try and cover it, I don't want her boyfriend to think I'm encouraging her. This is one place I don't want to be having a fight that is for sure. The man sitting next to her snaps. Damn he looks pissed, but she seems surprisingly unfazed by it all.

"Isabella Jonson." I hear her name called loud and clear then watch as the girl and guy stand up. Wow, what a beautiful name. I roll the name Isabella around in my head a few times to get the feel of it. When she stands I see she has long legs that go on for days, and a figure that is not fat and not skinny, just right I think. As they are walking down the hallway, Isabella stops and looks back at me. I think she's going to ask for my name or something, maybe even my phone number. I feel my back stiffening. Please don't do it with your boyfriend standing right there. I really don't need a fight here today. What does come out of her mouth is not at all what I expected.

"Do you like to eat Mexican? Because you're heating up my taco." I can't help the laugh that bubbles out of me. I would apologize to her boyfriend, but that chat up line is funny as fuck. I can hear everyone in the room laughing with me, as I watch her ass walk down the corridor to the courtroom.

Chapter Four

Ryker

I sit for all of three minutes before jumping to my feet and rushing down the same corridor. I want to see what is going on in the courtroom, and I know for a fact I can watch from the public viewing area. That is where all the paparazzi sat during my father's trial. I open the door as slowly and quietly as humanly possible to try and get in unannounced, but it would seem I'm shit out of luck when the dark, heavy wooden door makes a loud groaning sound. It feels like all the people in the room have turned to look at me.

I try to ignore all of their stares and keep my eyes downcast, as I shuffle my feet forward, like my ass is on fire and find a seat. Keeping every muscle in my body tense, I slowly lower myself hoping to God the seat doesn't make a sound, as I'm sure that would really look bad. Luckily I get seated without any more noise. Glancing around the room, I can see this courtroom is completely different than the ones at home.

This courtroom is all dark wood and ugly carpet, kind of how I would imagine a gentleman's club to look, just without the cigar smoke. Whereas, at home the courtrooms are big and full of light, they are inviting. This room is just dark and morbid. I feel intimidated just sitting in the public viewing box. I look over at the beautiful girl with the bottle green eyes and see that she is also looking at me. A small smile raises the side of my mouth, her eyes are mesmerizing. It's like looking into the bottom of an empty bottle and finding all the answers you need. I don't see any worry in her eyes about the current issue at hand. The fact being she is sitting in a courtroom and could possibly end up in jail. I'm not sure what she is here for, but she seems to have lawyered up, which means it's probably bad. It suddenly dawned on me that the guy who was next to her in the waiting area, is now sitting at the lawyers table and not in the viewing area. Maybe he isn't her boyfriend after all. I want to give myself a high five, but I know that in the current circumstances it wouldn't go down well and may make me look crazy. So I give myself a mental high five instead.

I try and keep my eyes locked with hers. For some strange reason, I want to give her my strength and protection. She has a fire inside that I want to keep lit, but also I can feel that she is hurting and needs my protection. Fuck, I need to hit myself in the head for even thinking such mushy shit. I'm in no position to protect this girl. Hell, I need my own protection first. Before I know what is happening, the court is coming to an end. The judges have given her 100 hours of community service and a last warning. That makes me think that she may have had a few warnings before. Not jumping to conclusions or anything, but she doesn't really seem like the type to have many run ins with the law. More the type to like sitting at home knitting with grandma.

Watching the judges leave, I glance over and see the lawyer/boyfriend march over to the girl, he has this pissed off look on his face. I would hazard a guess and say that didn't go the way he expected. A raised voice grabs my attention.

"It was only a speeding ticket," the female shrieks, sounding a bit like a pterodactyl dinosaur. So she is here for a speeding ticket, she must have had a few to land her in court. Damn, did the guy just say 100mph over the speed limit. Yep that will definitely land you in here. My dick jumps in my pants at the thought of this girl being a speed demon. If there is one constant in my life, it's my love of speed.

I shuffle back to the waiting area as I obviously can't get close to her with her bodyguard standing on duty, I need to try and come up with some way of finding out more about her. I find it a little sad-dening that she could walk out of here and I won't ever see her again. I watch as her and the guy walk down the corridor and out through the metal de-tector, and that's it, my chance is lost. I slide into the hard plastic waiting chairs again and take out my phone. Slipping headphones into my ears, I hit play and let Def Leppard, Love Bites, stream into my ears. I should have known with my luck, and the fates being the twisted bitches that they are, that the song is a warning. A warning I should have heeded.

Chapter Five

Isabella

E ven before we make it back to Remi's car, my phone is already ringing. I pluck it out of my purse while Devil Woman by Cliff Richard plays. Hearing the ring tone alone causes me to groan, I know it's my mother. Remi looks over at me and bursts out laughing, "Really, Issy, do you not think that is a bit much?" Rolling my eyes, I don't think it's anywhere near enough for that woman and he of all people should know that. But she only shows her really nasty side behind closed doors. Heaven forbid, she would never slap me in front of company, that stuff is done when no one else is around. I let the phone go to voicemail, I really don't need to speak to her right now.

Within seconds of me rejecting her call, Remi's phone is ringing. Raising it up so the screen is facing me, I see my mother's name flashing on it. Rolling my eyes again, he proceeds to answer it with his posh voice.

"Good afternoon, Mrs Jonson," he says into the phone, while still heading for his car. I trail behind him in the hope he will forget I'm here and just leave me. I don't mind grabbing a bus or taxi home. In fact, I use my car very little and usually choose public transport instead. I only use my car when it's needed, like for street racing or when I have to pick up one of my friends. Normally those friends are too snobby to ride the underground with me. I really don't see the point of driving in the city, when it can take an hour to do like six miles. On the underground that same six miles would only be a ten minute ride. Plus, I love to watch people while I'm riding public transport. I'm not going to lie, I've met some amazingly wonderful people along the way. But on the flip side, there's been some scary-arse people as well. However, knowing Remi, he will want me to go straight home and stay in my ivory tower.

Glancing over I see a big distance has opened up

between us. I wonder if I will be able ro turn around and bolt. Maybe I will go and sit in the courthouse and watch other strangers' court proceedings, and by strangers I mean one stranger in particular. It's odd, that I already miss his warm eyes and the sense of protection that he brought me in the courtroom. If I was ever going to have a Bonnie and Clyde moment, I'd want him to be the one with me.

"Stop dawdling and get in the car. Your mother is expecting you at home to discuss your community service," Remington III shouts at me, while I have my back to him looking at the courthouse. As much as Remi and I are friends, he will always be in my mother's pocket. The vision my mother holds of our families joining together, with me and him getting hitched and having little Remington the 4ths running around, is sickening to me. But I know that Remi is all for it, he just isn't as pushy as my mother. He wants me to come around to the idea by myself. Well I have news for both of them, hell will freeze over before that happens.

Taking a deep breath and making sure the iron rod is in place down my spine, I turn around with a huge smile on my face and say, "coming" in a sweet, sickly voice that no longer sounds like my own. Is it wrong that I was hoping for some jail time? At least there are other people in jail with you. Whereas, the jail I'm currently heading to is solely my own. The song Highway to Hell by AC/DC starts playing in my mind. I can feel my head start to nod along to the song and the next instant, I start humming the chorus. Music has always been my gateway. I can see Remi giving me a sideways glance out of the corner of his eye. He's never understood my need to burst into song, which is one of the reasons why we will never work.

Opening the door to his red Tesla X, my legs slide across the custom white leather as I get in. Remington III has had this car for over a year now and it still has that new car smell. It must be coming to the point where he will trade it in for a newer version, he doesn't keep cars for very long. Whereas, my car has junk all over it and smells like McDonalds and old socks, much to my mother's dismay. She's had the maids take it countless times to the valeting business down the road, who then bring it back sparkling clean and smelling like a pine forest. Not a nice pine forest, but a chemical one. I can't stand it and it doesn't take long before I fill it full of crap again. I like being surrounded by mess and chaos. It's the only thing in my life that I actually get to control.

I go to turn the radio on and listen to some music as the quietness in the electric car is awkward as fuck, but there are too many buttons for me to know which one swtiches the radio on and doesnt switch the car off. Knowing my luck I would hit the ejector seat and be tossed right out of the car.

Actually, that thought doesn't seem that bad an idea the more I think about it. Before I can ponder on that thought any more, the sound of a ringing phone blasts through the speakers of the car. Pushing a button on the steering wheel, Remi answers with his name, including the 3rd part. This causes an eye roll, and a small giggle to burst from me. It must be someone from the law firm as they start talking about paperwork. Not wanting to hear the conversation, I reach down into my bag and slip out my headphones. Since I still have the AC/DC song playing in my head, I decide to blast the actual song in my ears. I glance out of the window and watch as London flashes by. London has always been my home, but I haven't gotten to see much of it. When you're a wealthy Londoner, there are not many places you can hang out with friends, making the area seem small. I don't want to see the same places all the time, I want to experience it all.

Chapter Six

Ryker

Hours have passed and I'm still sitting in the same plastic chair. Most people have already been in and out of the court-room. Some come out happy, but mostly the people have come out looking dejected. I look around the room when the usher comes back out and sees I'm the last one left. Glancing up, I see him looking down at me. He looks worn out and despondent, in all honesty I would hate his job. I like a more hands on job, like building cars or motor-bikes. Writing and learning was never really my thing, I always struggled with it at school.

"Ready?" he asks, taking the paperwork of my income status from my hands and giving it a glance over. It makes me embarrassed for someone to truly know how poor I am. As my Memaw would say, I don't have two nickels to rub together. The only thing I have to my name is my Harley Davidson Softail slim. It's my pride and joy that my dad gifted me when I graduated high school, back when we had money. Before the financial crash that stole my father's life and in turn mine.

The bike is a beauty all unto itself, with custom made fenders, wide 'Hollywood' handlebars and a sleek black trim. The whole set up gives the bike more of a retro look. It may look like a classic, but it's engine is brand spanking new. The brute power of the bike comes from its 1690cc twin-cam v-twin heart, creating top speeds of a mind blowing 150 mph.

The bike means everything to me. It's all I was able to send over from America, the only thing that was in my name and not my dad's. Everything else had been repossessed and auctioned off to pay back his debts from the stock market crashing. As he had no living relatives, the lawyers and state sent me here to my mom. I would have rather stayed on the streets and earned my own way, back home. But my mother petitioned the courts in America to have me, so they sent me over. I'm sure she would've been none the wiser of my father's death if she'd still been receiving payments from him. But I hadn't known any of this until after he died.

I slowly rise up from my seat, causing my leather jacket to groan in protest from being sat in the same spot for so long. I follow the usher down the corridor in the same way I had watched the girl from earlier do. Thinking about her brings a slight smile to my face. She has been a light on this dark day. I'm kicking myself for not getting her number, but I didn't want to start anything with her boyfriend/lawyer there. Not that I can't hold my own in a fist fight, but I don't think a courthouse is really the place to be fighting. That shit should be kept on the streets.

I follow the usher into the courtroom and take my seat in the box. Glancing up, I see that it's the same judges the girl had earlier.

"State your name and age," says the female judge while still looking at the paperwork piled up high on her desk.

"Ryker Allen Williams, twenty six years old, born May 21st 1994, ma'am," I respond loud and clear, I'm not ashamed to be here.

"Oh! You must be American?" the female judge responds with a fluttering of her eyelashes.

"Yes, Alabama ma'am," I say proudly while holding her gaze. I can tell she is flirting with me and I'm going to use that to my advantage. What Southern man hasn't used his charm to get himself out of sticky situations before? I'm sure if the parking attendant had been a female, I could have smooth-talked my way out of the parking ticket I ended up with. But I'm never that lucky, it was a grumpy old man that decided to stand there and give me a lecture on how it wasn't the American's that saved Britain in the Second World War, and that the British could have won without us sticking our noses in. Apparently that is all American's are good for, sticking their noses in where they're not wanted. He then started droning on about how people would elect an orange Cheeto to run their country. By that point I couldn't take it anymore, so I just took the ticket and walked off. To be honest, that lecture alone was punishment enough in my eyes.

By the time the 'reminder to pay' had arrived in the mail, I couldn't afford to pay the fine, which is how I find myself sitting in this wonderful courtroom. Yes, that was sarcasm and I can feel my eyes rolling at my own internal monologue.

"I have never been to Alabama, many other states, but never Alabama. Ok, I'm sure you know why you're here, a ticket for parking in a no parking zone outside a hospital," she says as if in sympathy for me.

"Yes ma'am." That was what I had done. I look down in embarrassment. Dad would be so ashamed of me finding myself in this position right now.

"The court is ruling that you must pay the £150 parking fine. I see on your paperwork that you don't have a steady form of income, you can work out a payment plan with the usher," she says with a gentle smile. "Court dismissed." I let out a huge sigh of relief as the judges walked out of the room. I can't believe how different that was from the girl's case earlier today. They had been so harsh to her, not kind like they were to me.

The usher walks over and gestures for me to follow him out of the courtroom and into a side office. Hopefully this guy understands I can't afford to pay much, but at least they aren't taking my bike.

I take a seat in front of the gray plastic desk that seems to have more paperwork on it than stationary. He takes my file from the top of the pile and opens it. It's not a very big file, maybe three or four bits of paper. That makes sense as I haven't had many runs in with the law, this being my only time. I try and keep my nose clean whenever I can.

"Shoot, the direct debit paperwork isn't here. One second while I just go and grab it off the printer," he says more to himself then to me, as he rises to his feet and strides out the door. I can hear his steps as he heads down the corridor. Looking around the office I see that it is piled high with different cardboard boxes, spilling paperwork everywhere. I'm not sure this room could be classified as an office, more like a storage room with a desk and chair in it. Dad's office back in America had been huge with a massive mahogany desk that was clear of any paperwork, just a top spec computer on top and behind it sat a huge leather chair. However, the biggest difference had been that dad's office was full of natural light with its wall of floor-to-ceiling windows. The office I was currently occupying had no windows at all, just a little hanging light overhead.

As my eyes trail over the desk I spot a huge file sitting on the top of a pile of paperwork, in fact I think it's two files stapled together. Glancing at the edge of it, I see the name JONSON, Isabella. I wonder if this file has her contact number in, or is that a little bit too stalkerish. What would I even say if I got her number? *Hey it's me, the guy you met in court, the one you were using the cheesy ass pick up lines on? Well, I hope you don't mind, but I kinda stole your contact number out of your court file.* It's not exactly the best, is it? Fuck it, I'll work out what to say when I hit that bridge.

Glancing behind me I see there is still no sign of the usher, I ever so slowly stand while simultaneously reaching over to lift open the cover of the file. Just as my hand is about to brush over it, my ass slams back down onto the seat when I see the usher heading back into the room with his nose in the paperwork he's holding. Slowly I release the breath I've been holding, I hope the usher doesn't see how flustered I am. What the hell had I been thinking? I'm sure it's a criminal offense to go snooping in another person's personal court details. I need to sort my head out and stop thinking about a girl I hardly know. What would have happened if I had been seen? I can't be taking risks like this, there is too much resting on my shoulders.

Chapter Seven

Isabella

Driving up the long driveway to my house is always daunting, hell even coming through the large gate is. The raw iron gates are black and have a mandala type of design on them, and where they join together there is a metal circle with a J in the middle. If my parents had asked my opinion on the gates before they had paid thousands of pounds for them, I would have told them that they are gaudy and over the top. Anyone would think people are trying to constantly break into our family home with the size of the gates and the razor wire over the surrounding brick wall, but it's all just for show. I always try to come through the service entrance, as one, I can use one of the maid codes, and two, it's smaller and more inconspicuous.

Again the Darth Vader Imperial Death Match comes into my head, this time I decide to vocalize it. "Dum dum dum dum de dum dum de dum." I try to make my voice sound as deep as possible. I notice a side glance from Remi, but other than that he keeps facing forward.

"Come on, it's not that bad. You're being a bit of a drama llama," he responds like he is sick and tired of this same conversation. I just humph back in return. He brings the car around the circular driveway, which has a fountain sitting in the middle with angels spitting water out of their trumpets. Many drunken parties have ended up with me in the fountain. I once asked a plumber if he could come over and make it so the water was flowing out of the angel's nipples, but he hung up the phone on me. Maybe one day I will get to do that, I would die to see the look on my parents' faces. Mind you, they would have to remove their heads from up their own arses to even notice the fountain had changed and I don't see that happening anytime soon.

Well it's time to face the music. I turn my head to Remi, maybe he will come inside and be my back up against my mother. She won't hit me in front of company. She doesn't care about the employed help seeing her as they have all signed NDA's and can't speak a word of it outside of this house. "You coming inside?" I ask timidly hoping to God he says yes, but he will only come in if my mother has already invited him. He nods his head back with a slight blush raising up his neck, like he knows that I'm thinking about how much he is controlled by my mother. He reaches for the door handle and pushes it open. The huge breath I had been holding rushes out of me, knowing she can't touch me while he is there is a big relief. I will just have to watch my back after he's gone, or hopefully he will make her drink herself to sleep. Fingers crossed.

The maid must have been waiting for us to arrive back as when I reach the top of the stairs the front door opens. She looks down at the floor, trying to not make eye contact. The last maid I became friends with had been sacked on the spot. So I make it my personal mission not to interact with any of them anymore. I felt terrible for Trudi losing her job when she had a baby at home and was already living on the breadline.

As I enter the large foyer, which could probably house a small country, I take my coat off and hand it over to the maid. This part of the house always reminds me of a museum, with its high ceiling and marble floors, a big circular stairway with a gold banister and a grand piano underneath it. The irony is that no one in this house can even play the piano, so it just sits there like an expensive ornament. Most families have pictures of their family or trinkets on display, but we have a piano and God ugly art.

I can feel my phone vibrating in my pocket. I want to take it out and check who it is, but knowing my luck my mother would choose that moment to jump out from wherever she is hiding. The maid raises her hand and points to the library, like she can hear my thoughts on the location of my mother. Great, she is in the room with the most items that she can throw at me. Note to self, don't let Remi leave your side whilst in the library.

Remi knows the way around this house as if it were his own, he's spent more time in the other rooms of the house than I have. I try to keep myself in rooms I consider safe; like my bedroom, the kitchen, and laundry room. Those are the rooms that neither of my parents venture in to, plus there are always staff working in them. I don't know if my mother knows those rooms even exist.

I follow 'The Third' into the room. I call him The Third when he goes into that mode that he uses to deal with my mother, the polite yet submissive one. I take a deep breath, and make sure my back is straight as I walk in behind him, eyes cast down in a timid manner. I have learned that if I keep quiet, nod when needed and keep my eyes down cast then these beratings go alot faster.

The room is huge with floor to ceiling, dark wood shelving containing every book imaginable. Hardback, paperback, leather bound and on any topic you could think of. Well all but one. I'm sure if my mother knew the types of books I read she would clutch her pearls and send me to a nunnery. Where books are concerned, I'm all for the darker and dirtier stuff. Erotica and reverse harem are my kind of kink. I tried some of the lighter things I had read with my ex-boyfriend and let's just say it didn't end well. According to him handcuffs are for criminals and not for the bedroom. He then proceeded to get on top in the missionary position and grunt away. Sex with him had been boring and very vanilla. I have always wanted more than vanilla, I just need to find it.

Before I even realised that I was daydreaming, fingers were being clicked in front of my face. I have always hated my mother for doing that to me or to anyone. It's just plain rude. I swing my eyes back around to my mother and see annoyance flaring in her eyes. She doesn't like not being listened to, especially by me, someone she believes to be below her and easy to control.

"Do you agree or not Isabella, this childish behaviour has to stop. I just can't take it much longer?" my mother says directly at me, with a sharp look in her eyes. Crap, my brain scrambles back as to what she has been saying while I was daydreaming about bad sex no less. I look over at Remi and see him nod his head slightly, I guess to try and hide the helpful gesture from my mother.

"Mm-hmm" I respond back, not fully knowing what I'm agreeing too, but I need out of this room. The stale cigar smoke is starting to make me feel queasy, and the leather high back seats are not my idea of comfy. The whole time I have been in this room, my phone has been vibrating like crazy in my pocket. I could see the exit, it felt so close but so far away, all at the same time.

"It is either a yes or no," she responds over pronouncing the words yes and no. I know it's a not so subtle stab at my lazy response before.

"Yes," I say back before she can carry on the lecture she is about to give about correct pronunciation of words.

"Fine," she harumphs back. "Be gone, I need to finish reading this," and just like that we are dismissed from the room.

I let my legs carry my arse as fast as they can back into the foyer, as if the hounds of hell are nipping at my heels. Running up the curved staircase as fast as I can, I grab my phone out of my pocket as I go.

"I will pick you up tomorrow at eight in the morning to take you to your community service," I hear Remi shout up the staircase as I go, but the phone in my hand has the majority of my attention at the moment. A text suggesting a night out is all my brain processes.

Fuck yeah! Just what I need, I think to myself as I reach my room. A night out of my mind and what's the worst that can happen, right?

Chapter Eight

Isabella

I feel as though I'm dressed perfectly in a boutique, sequin print, bodycon dress with long mesh sleeves and a hem that reaches to my mid thigh, showcasing my long legs. Being 5'7 means I have legs that seem to go on for days. My pastel pink hair is curled to perfection, and styled so it falls over one side of my face. My make-up is minimal with light pink lip gloss and mascara. All in all I look damn hot. Now I just need to get out of the house without my parents seeing or every cop will be called to hunt me down before I can get in anymore trouble. It wouldn't be the first time my parents had used the police force to bully me back home.

Keeping my heels loose in my hands, I slowly open my door to take a peek out. It doesn't creak open anymore after I learnt to use a bit of lube on the hinges. I quietly opened the door up just enough for me to slip out and close it softly again. Getting down the stairs is the easy part, it's getting past the study next to the front door that is the hard part. Suddenly I hear the sound of approaching footsteps. I know it's not my mother as her heels make more of a clicking sound on the tiled floor. Releasing a breath I had been holding, I see it's one of the maids.

"Miss Isabella, what are you doing?" the maid asks in a quiet voice. She must be new as I don't recognise her face.

"Ummmm, sneaking out?" I say with a confused look on my face, she is definitely new. All the maids here would have known what I was doing and that after today I would be on lockdown, which meant they would have to report my comings and goings to mother and father.

"Miss, you do know your parents aren't here, right?" she says glancing around as if to make sure she isn't being watched. "They have gone to a charity event this evening and are not due back till later." Before she has even finished the sentence I'm already jumping and shouting into the air.

"Whoop Whoop," I yell with a fist in the air, like the rebel from The Breakfast Club. With new vigor to leave the house, I jump down the steps two at a time. Glancing back up I see the maid give a little wink in my direction. Well well well, looks like I may have someone in my corner again. However, I remind myself it's not like I can be-friend her. I ran into the garage, grabbing my car keys in the process and slid into my beautiful car, which was a birthday present from my dad, much to my mother's anger. She doesn't like my father spending this much money on me. She would ra-ther he spend it buying her new flashy toys and jewels. I slip the keys into the ignition, and as my Aston Martin Vanquish starts, the engine purrs to life. The vibrations slide up my thighs and cause adrenaline to flow through my body.

Clicking the button to open up the garage door, I get impatient at how long it takes, so I sit with my foot on the accelerator pedal, causing a roar to come from the car. I only get to do this when the mighty Lords of the Manor are not here. If they were here, I would be in deep shit right now. How-ever, they are not, so I'm going to do what I want.

Once the garage door is open I smile, knowing I'm going to enjoy this. Keeping the revs high, I slam the car into gear while dropping the handbrake.

This causes the wheels to spin and shoot forward when they finally get traction. Gazing in the rearview mirror I see two big black lines on the garage floor, left over from my wheel spin. Oh well, shit happens. I'm sure one of the maids will have it cleaned by the time I get home. I will have to find out which one and slip them some extra cash as a thank you for cleaning up my mess and covering for my arse.

Speeding down the driveway, I see someone has already opened the gate for me so I don't have to stop. Once I reach the main road I bring my speed down to within the speed limit. Would hate to get a trigger happy copper again and end up with another speeding ticket. The speakers in my car start blasting my ringtone.

"Answer that," I say towards my dashboard as I know the car speaker is somewhere in that direction. The ringing cuts off and a voice comes through with a heavy bass music behind it.

"Criminal, where are you?" my friend Conor shouts at me over the music behind him.

"On my way, ETA 10 mins," I shout back so he can hear me.

Pulling up outside the club, I climb out of the car and hand my keys to the valet. I look over at the entrance where Conor is standing outside waiting for me, leaning against the column with a cigarette in his hand. Conor and I have been friends for a long time. He is like a brother to me, always has my back against the paparazzi and the social climbers. He's a really decent guy, but we both learnt after one drunk and sloppy night that there isn't any romantic spark between us.

"The party girl is here. Let's go beautiful," Conor says while wrapping his arm around my waist. Conor's real name is Dorran, but as he's always looked like the Irish MMA fighter Conor McGregor, the name just kind of stuck. Plus, they are both Irish. I said a long time ago that he should have DNA tested as they could be identical twins. Still holding my waist, he leads me inside to the party.

As I walk through the doors, I see the majority of people are wearing orange jumpsuits with black numbers on the back. I turn to face Conor and smack his chest using the back of my hand. Oh God this is mortifying, I can't believe he's arranged this.

"How could you, you traitor," I say with a lifted smile and a gleam in my eye. He looks back at me with a huge grin, like he gets off on my embarrassment.

"Drinks," I yell at the top of my lungs. The room responds back with a "Hoot Hoot". The people in this room are my crew, my gang. Don't get me wrong, they would sell their own grandmothers to please their parents or to climb the social ladder. But these are the only friends I have ever known.

In the next moment I'm handed a drink and a shot. The drink is my favourite, a Mojito, but the shot, oh these guys are starting early and plan on me getting shitfaced. This shot in particular is my nemesis, the Jäger bomb. It comes with two glasses, a tall glass full of red bull and a shot glass inside filled with Jägermeister. I have many lost nights because of this drink. Oh well, bottoms up, as we say here. As soon as I have swallowed the burning liquid down my throat, a "hoot hoot" is shouted out by everyone in the club. No faster have I turned back to the bar, there is another Jäger bomb waiting for me. Here goes nothing, I think to myself as Locked Up by Akon blasts through the speakers causing the floor to vibrate with its loud bass.

Chapter Nine

Isabella

Oh God, I think I'm dying. My head feels like it's being caved in and I'm pretty sure my brain is floating in alcohol. How did I even get home last night? What I thought was the pounding in my head is actually someone knocking on my bedroom door. Without having to say a word my door is pushed open and Remi comes striding in.

"You look like absolute shit right now. Get up and get showered," he yells while tugging my covers off. "You have community service in an hour." He probably isn't yelling, but any noise above a whisper sounds like shouting right now.

It's a good job I wasn't naked under my duvet because if I was he sure as hell would be getting an eye full right now. "Uhhhh, did you at least bring me a cup of tea?" I say in my most whiny voice. Even my own voice is hurting my ears.

"Get out of bed and you will find out," he responds while opening my curtains. Holy hellfire that is too damn bright.

"I'm melting," I respond in the most dramatic demonic voice I can muster, while holding my hands up to cover my eyes. "Can you carry me to the bathroom? I think my legs have stopped working?" I say with my sweetest smile in place. He comes over to me, getting ready to pick me up. Suddenly he backs away. Crap, is one of my boobs hanging out again? It sometimes happens when I wear a strappy top like this.

"Fucking hell, your breath could set this house on fire! No, I'm staying well away till you brush your damn teeth!" He says while taking a seat on my makeup stool.

"Jackass, that is not a nice thing to say to a lady," I say right back to him, while cupping my hand over my mouth to take a whiff. "But this time I shall let you off as you're right, it smells like something died in there."

Heading over to my en-suite, I open the door and head straight for the shower. Flipping the switches to get the shower going and to the perfect temperature. The various shower heads spurt into action and steam starts rising around the room. Heading over to the control panel next to the vanity mirror, I hit my favourite hangover playlist and a soothing melody starts playing around the room. It helps to get my blood pumping and removes the last of the sleepy fog from around my brain. Slipping my clothes off, I head over to the walk in shower, which is now the perfect temperature to get in. The pressure of the water from the different outlets feels amazing, like having a full body massage. Releasing a deep breath I can feel the last of my hangover finally dissipate, I must have been on the dance floor for most of the night as my muscles are feeling all sorts of achy today.

Grabbing my sponge, I squeeze a liberal amount of sweet smelling shower foam and run it all over my body. Scrubbing the last of the alcohol from my skin gives me that beautiful refreshing feeling. Now to tackle the nest of hair on my head. Just as I'm rubbing shampoo on my scalp I hear the bathroom door open and a waft of cold air enter. Glancing over my shoulder, I see Remi standing there. Lucky for me, the shower has a half wall so all he can see is the top of my back. Otherwise, I would sure as hell be yelling at him right now.

Giving him a pointed look, as if to say, 'what the hell are you doing in my bathroom while I'm naked?' he starts to speak to me with both his hands raised up in a peaceful gesture.

"I knocked and called your name, but you didn't hear me. We need to leave, like now to make it on time," he says while grabbing my towel and placing it on the half wall.

"OK," I respond, while moving my hands in a shooing gesture. Grabbing the fluffy soft towel off the wall, I try to keep my back to him so he doesn't get an eye full of my boobs. If the pink blush creeping up his face is anything to go by, he may have had at least some side boob. Oh well, I'm sure he will get over it.

When I re-enter my bedroom Remi hands me some paperwork, I glance over it while entering my walk-in wardrobe. The top white sheet of A4 is a list of clothes not to wear. Anything that could link you to a possible gang, or even football team is out. No expensive designer clothes or accessories, as they could be robbed or stolen. No footwear that could be deemed a weapon. Oh damn, I had planned on wearing my 6 inch heels while I go and collect rubbish from the side of the motorway. The list doesn't really help me with what to wear. After a quick glance around, I settle on a pair of black leggings and a wooly off one shoulder top in mint green. To round off my ensemble, I grab my shiny black high top Doc Martens with flowers all over them. They are kind of like my guilty pleasure and I'm 100% sure that if I didn't hide them away in my wardrobe my mother would have binned them long ago. I quickly rub some oil over my locks and head back into my bedroom, nodding at Remi to signal I'm ready to go.

Chapter Ten

Isabella

Well this isn't so bad, I think to myself sarcastically when Remi drops me off at the meeting point for community service. I hadn't wanted to bring my own car in case something happened to it while I was busy, and not only that but it would draw unwanted attention to me. I'm not going to lie, this place is scary as fuck. Big, tall, flat buildings are all crammed together, there must be about eight of them all around here. People are shouting at each other, there's garbage everywhere, even furniture, including couches, are just dumped around. Graffiti marks every wall, from swear words to gang names. Don't get me wrong, I'm not against graffiti, it can be a form of art, but this is just needless vandalism. While I'm looking around at my surroundings I feel a tap on my shoulder causing me to jump in the air and let out a girly scream. Once I see who it is, I try to steady my heartbeat and get oxygen back into my lungs. "Crazy shitballs, you scared the crap out of me," I say to the lady standing directly in front of me.

"Did you read the paperwork that was supplied to you? If you had, you would have clearly known not to use that type of language around here." Just as she finishes the sentence, a door about two floors up opens and a screaming woman walks out holding a man by his ear.

"Get your fucking lazy, shaky, shaggy ass out my fucking door," she screams at him. I raise a hand to my mouth to cover the laugh that's dying to come out. But God only knows what would happen. After the angry woman has retreated back into her flat, I turn to face the lady with a grin on my face and say, "You were saying?"

The lady, who I can only imagine is the person in charge of us hooligans, just huffs and walks away.

"You must be new," I hear coming from a voice to my left. I look over to see a boy, he must be no older than seventeen. He has greasy black hair that hangs over his eyes, and is wearing baggy jeans with big holes over the knees and a faded Guns and Roses t-shirt.

"Is it that obvious?" I ask while raising my shoulders. He doesn't look scary or have a threatening manner. In fact the more I look at him, the more I see his shoulders are hunched over, as if he is trying to make himself seem as small as possible.

"Yeah, it is. You have that shiny new toy look, but a few hours around here with the dregs of society and that sparkle will dim in your eyes," Wow, that doesn't sound foreboding at all.

"Ok then, thanks for the head up," I say looking around for any signs of instruction, but everyone just seems to be milling around with nothing to do. If I have to do this for 100 hours, I'm going to go crazy. I'm not exactly in favour of hard labour, I just seem to find myself getting in trouble when I have nothing to do. My grandma used to say to me, the devil makes work for idle hands. She was right in more ways than one. It's not even like there is anywhere for me to sit down either, the metal benches have been ripped from their bases and all that's left is large metal poles sticking from the ground. Yeah, because that isn't a safety hazard right there.

"Everyone gather around," the stern lady from before shouts and starts waving her hands in a come here gesture. I slowly make my way over to her.

I don't want to seem too eager to get started and so I force my legs to move slowly, even though it's killing me to stand around and not do anything. Maybe, I should sell that idea to the government as a great punishment idea, I'm sure the reoffending rates would drop drastically. I know I wouldn't be reoffending if they had me doing nothing but standing for over one hundred hours.

"So, the job this week will be to clear up this area for the council. A skip is being delivered today for all the rubbish and broken furniture. All the graffiti needs cleaning off the walls before we can paint them. The ground needs sweeping, and the park needs pressure washing. I will pair you up and delegate each pair a task. You are to do that task unless I instruct otherwise. There will be no breaks unless I tell you, and there will be NO fighting, do I make myself clear?" I nod my head in fear that I will end up bearing the brunt of her anger if I don't respond in some way. She reminds me of my old headmistress, she was stern and took no shit too.

"When I call your names, walk forward and collect the necessary gear to keep you safe. As most of you are my regulars, you know the rules. If the newbies have read the packs supplied to them then they will also know the rules." Moving my eyes as fast as I can without giving them whiplash, I train them on the floor, but I can feel her eyes burning holes in the top of my head. Damn, I bet that was in all the paperwork Remi handed me this morning. The one that I didn't read and I kinda just threw on my bed. Fuckity fuck fuck fuck.

I hear my name called and slide over to the woman in charge as she hands me a bucket, sponge and some yellow plastic gloves. "You're on graffiti duty with Zoe."

I give her my megawatt smile and respond, "Yay me." I hope she can hear the sarcasm in my voice.

"Maybe next time you won't commit a crime, that way you won't have to put in the time," she says with as much sarcasm as I gave her. I feel like that should be her slogan then she could walk around with it on a t-shirt and just point at it instead of saying it. If only I had committed the crime, maybe then I wouldn't be so bitter about being here. Maybe I should stop lending people my car.

Loaded up with the supplies she handed me, I walked over to the first wall. "This is a fucking pointless job, why does it need washing first? Why can't we just paint over it," I mutter under my breath.

"It's because of the grease in the paints, it makes it harder to paint over. We have to wash the grease off first, so it doesn't seep through when it's re-painted. But to be honest I'm surprised these walls are still standing with the amount of paint on them. They've been painted at least eight times since I've been here. Hi I'm Zoe," she says while extending her hand to me.

I raise my own hand to shake hers, "Hi, I'm Isabella, but call me Issy," I respond with a smile. Zoe looks pretty easy going. She's dressed in skin tight blue wash jeans, with a blue wife beater. Her hair seems to be a light brown colour from what I can see poking out of the bottom of her beanie, and her eyes are a bright blue colour. But it's her smile that captures my attention the most, it's warm and welcoming. Compared to the other people around here that all look sad and drawn out, her smile stands out from the crowd.

"You're new here right?" she asks while putting her rubber gloves on.

"Yeah, this is my first time doing community service," I say while trying to wrestle my own gloves on. How did she make it look so damn easy?

"Here, it helps if you blow into them first, it kinda helps unstick them," she pulls the rubber glove away from me and blows into it. Once she has given it back, my hand just slides right into it.

"You have to teach me more, Master Yoda," I respond with awe lacing through my words.

"Stick with me my young Padawan and I will teach you all I know," she responds with a laugh at the end. By the end of our banter, I can feel the corners of my lips rising into a smile. I think I may have just found a new friend to do my community service with.

Chapter Eleven

Ryker

Rising from the couch, where I have been having a time out after spending all morning cleaning the house following another one of Mom's hissy fits, I glance out of the small apartment window. There is so much grime on the outside of the window that I just can't get to, making it so we can barely see out of it. But I can see that the park area is full of people. Oh yeah, that community service that Zoe is doing starts today. I was lucky to just get a fine, or I would be down there too. Maybe when she gets her lunch break

I'll head down and take her something to eat as I know she will have forgotten to take her lunch with her. She has more than enough on her plate dealing with six children.

Zoe and I have a strange relationship going on. We dated for a few months when I first arrived here and she helped me with finding my feet. Then we realised we were only fuck buddies and nothing more, there wasnt really any chemisty between us. We have never let our history come between us though and we still remain friends, which is good because she is one of the only people I can trust around here.

Heading into the kitchen I grab the sliced bread from the counter and ham from the refrigerator then get prepping on making the sandwich. Shooting off a quick text to Zoe, I ask what time her lunch will be, before I head back over to the window. Some of the stories I've heard about community service have been brutal; people getting beat-up, stabbed and one guy even got shot. Around here, if you are caught on the wrong side of the estate, even for community service, it can end badly. The state doesn't take that into consideration when handing out community service as a sentence.

After hearing back from Zoe that it's lunch time, I grab a few packets of crisps and some water bottles then head out of the front door. Nothing about these buildings are special, in fact they are some of the worst I have ever seen in my life. The smell is what hit you first, they stink of sweaty bodies and piss. The noise is second to the smell, there are always people shouting and talking in the halls, mostly gang members. The walls are covered in graffiti and most of the lights are broken or the bulbs have been stolen. Furniture litters the hallway causing such a fire hazard it's scary to even think about. Living on the seventh floor with no elevators means a long trek down the stairs, but it could be worse, I could live on the twentieth. I nod my head back as a silent show of respect to the guys in the stairwell, they know I have their backs so they have mine. But these guys ain't the type you want to stop and have a friendly chit chat with. As you will only be dragged into their drama. Reaching the ground floor, I jump the last few steps that bring me straight into the park area. Within a few long strides I'm wrapping my arms around her front and I feel her body tense under mine, so I whisper hello in her ear and instantly I feel her relax. Looking up, I'm taken aback by the girl Zoe is talking to.

"Hey, it's you," I say with shock in my voice. I genuinely never thought I would see her again.

"Hey yourself," she says back with a wicked grin on her face, a pure look of mischief.

"What no cheesy pick up lines today?" I see her

eyes quickly flash over to Zoe's face with a hint of shame. Oh shit, she must think I'm dating Zoe.

"Ok, I'll leave you guys to your lunch," She says while glancing at my hand, eyeballing the sandwich and chips. She turns away from us and takes out her cell phone, her fingers fly over the keyboard, no doubt updating her tweets or something as pointless as that. I watch her ass as she walks over to another building and brushes some muck away with her hand before sitting on the ground. At least it hasn't been raining today so the floor isn't wet. She sits with her phone glued to her hand, capturing all her attention.

Swinging my eyes back to Zoe, I see the shit eating grin across her face. I raise my eyebrows in question before handing over the sandwich.

"So pray tell, how do you know Miss fancy pants over there?" Zoes asks while cocking her hip to one side. "You have absolutely met her before and I'm just wondering where. It's not like you two hang out in the same circles."

"In court yesterday, she sat across from me with her rich snooty boyfriend. I think she was trying to piss him off by throwing pick up lines my way." I try to stop the smile from growing at the memory, but I can't help it. Even just thinking about her and the way she lit up the waiting room, all with just her cheeky smile, beautiful face and electric personality gets me hard.

Zoe's eyes light up with understanding and we both swing our eyes over to where Isabella is sitting on the floor still staring at her phone.

"Follow me," Zoe says with a wink and starts striding over to where Isabella is sitting. When she hears us approaching, she raises her head from her phone to look cautiously at us. It's like she is worried we might be coming over to start trouble. Zoe is oblivious to Isabella's facial expression because she just jumps straight in.

"Issy, did you bring any lunch with you?" Zoe asks like they are best friends.

"Uh no, I didn't know we had to," Isabella responds shyly as if she is embarrassed about forgetting a basic need.

"Girl, that's ok. I forgot as well, was way too busy getting the kids ready for school. Ryker here," she says while pointing her head in my direction, "made me some and I want to share it with you."

Isabella jumps to her feet. "Oh no. Thank you, but you don't have to do that for me," she says back to Zoe. I'm starting to get the feeling I'm watching a tennis match happening with all the backwards and forwards going on.

"It's no issue, I want to share with you. If Mrs Trunchbull gets her way we would be worked to the bone with no lunch. So let's sit down and enjoy it." While the conversation carried on in front of me, I was stuck to the spot. She looks so beautiful today, with her less formal clothes on. She carries an air of peace about herself, not like when she was waiting in court with her back as straight as a rod. No, today she is slightly more slumped over, looking completely at ease.

Seeing her and Zoe sit on the floor, I follow behind. I can feel her eyes on me so I raise my own to her and bring out the grin that makes girls pant for more. I know I'm not bad looking. This life here has changed me, I'm more ripped and have a lot more tattoos than I did when I left the States. I think if my dad saw me now he wouldn't recognize me. But you know what they say, we have to adapt to our surroundings to survive and that's what I did.

I hand her my sandwich. "Here take this, I can make another one when I head back up stairs."

"Thank you!" She responds with that blinding smile. "Wait, you live here?"

"Yeah, this block behind me." Lifting my hand up, I use my thumb to point behind me, indicating the building I'm talking about.

"Oh ok, is that how you two know each other?" Isabella asks.

"Yeah, this guy moved over here from America and I felt sorry for him as he had no idea how to deal with this world, so I helped hook him up and get him sorted," replies Zoe. I can see Isabella glancing between us and I'm internally begging Zoe not to bring up the sex part when she continues talking. "We tried dating but there was no chemistry between us, so we stayed as fuck buddies." Oh fuck, there it is. I quickly raise my eyes up to see what Isabella's face will show me, but she has her eyes locked on the ground. Well, this just got weird as hell.

"Alright, I'm heading back. Your lunch will be finished soon." I jump up to my feet like my ass is on fire.

"Thank you for the sandwich, " Isabella responds quickly.

"You are most welcome," I say walking backwards a few steps. Turning around I stride back to my building. When I get to the door, I turn around for one last glance and I see her and Zoe deep in conversation. I don't know how she does it, but it's like everyone else lights up in her presence and the world seems less dark.

As I'm heading up to the second floor someone steps in my path, blocking the rest of the way up. I look up to find out who the offender is, I have a bad rep around these areas now. I have learnt the hard way to not take shit, or they will beat the ever loving crap out of you. My shoulders relax when I see it's only Dave, he's the head gang leader around here and you definitely don't want to mess with him. I had done a few favors for him and earned his respect. It's not a story I want to think about very often and it changed me, but needs must. I couldn't take the beatings anymore. Not when it was ten on one.

"What's up Dave?" I ask not really giving a shit about what this fucker has to say, I just wanted to head back to the apartment and watch out the window like a crazy stalker. The need to see her again is driving me, like ants over my skin.

"There's a hand over tonight, I want you to be there when the deal is done. I don't trust these rich arseholes." I don't trust any of them, including him but I'm not about to point that out.

"Yeah, I can be there, just text me the details." It hurts that this is my life now, but I made that choice and I would do it again, to protect the girls.

"Did the courts come down on you hard?" He asks while moving himself against the bannister. He got the answer he wanted from me, or he wouldn't have moved out of the way. He would still be trying to get me to agree.

"Slap on the wrist and a fine," is all I say as I make my way past him.

"If you need the money, I've got a job for you," he shouts up the stairs as I reach my floor. I don't respond, I don't want his dirty money. Protection for my family, yes, but not drug money. Running down the corridor and jumping over trash, I have the key already in my hand waiting for the door. Jamming it into the lock, I fling the door open and slam it shut, even that noise wouldn't force my mother to wake up from her drug induced coma. I dash to the window and look down, yep I can see Zoe and Isabella working on the same wall as before. They seem to be laughing and joking, so everything must be fine. I just hope they are not laughing and joking about my dick size, as i know that is exactly what Zoe would do just to wind me up. She's probably telling Issy that it's tiny, and most probably wiggling her pinky finger while doing it. But we both know that's a lie. I'm rather proud of my dick size, and it's not like I've had any complaints.

Chapter Twelve

Isabella

After Ryker's awkward and rather abrupt departure, Zoe and I finished our lunch and got called back to work. The sandwich he gave me tasted nice and certainly helped with the hangover. I had felt so stupid for not reading the paperwork properly and not bringing a packed lunch with me. Maybe if I hadn't been so groggy this morning I may have questioned where my lunch would be coming from. Oh well, crisis averted.

The shock I felt seeing him had been strange and

unexpected. When I had said those chat up lines in court I hadn't actually expected to ever see him again. It was only after the initial shock wore off that I had felt the tingles run up and down my body. Watching him wrap himself around Zoe had been like having a bucket of ice cold water dumped on me. Then they had to kick me while I was down and tell me they had been together before, sexually no less.

All day Zoe had been like a proper friend, asking me loads of questions and telling me all about her life. If I wanted to keep her as a friend then I had to rememeber, you don't fuck where you sleep. In other words don't fuck your friend's ex-boyfriends. Believe you me that shit stinks!

It was about mid-afternoon and the day had gone surprisingly fast. One hundred hours would be a doozy as long as I have Zoe to keep me entertained. We finished cleaning the first wall and then were starting on the one next to it when we heard a huge commotion behind us.

I look over my shoulder with the sponge still raised up in my hand and see about fifty people heading towards us with microphones and cameras. They all seem to be shouting my name. Fuck sake, it's the paparazzi, how the hell did they find me? Looking around quickly, there is nowhere for me to go. No buildings I can safely hide in. Plus, Remi had dropped me here, I didn't even have a car to find shelter in.

The shouting gets louder as they close in and it won't be long until they are all on me, like the vultures they are. I glance over at Zoe with pleading eyes and she looks just as taken aback by the hoards of people stampeding towards us. In the blink of an eye Zoe has jumped in front of me and is using herself as a human shield. Before my brain can take in any more details a sleek black motorbike appears in front of Zoe. All my muscles are tensed and ready for action. What action I'm not really sure yet. There is no protection here for me from the paparazzi. Normally there are bouncers or hired help to clear the way, but this time I'm on my own.

When the rider takes his helmet off I see it's Ryker. Releasing the breath I had been holding, I grab the helmet he is holding out to me and drag it over my head in record time. Swinging my leg over the bike, I feel myself slide forward against his back. I'm too scared to even think about the ramifications of this! I watch as Ryker leans over to grab a second, slightly smaller helmet from a side bag on the bike, while whispering something in Zoe's ear. She gives him a sharp nod and next thing I know he is gunning the engine while I grip on for dear life. I have the helmet pushed up against his back and my thighs are gripping him as tight as humanly possible.

I can see London flying past us as we drive down the busy roads. I can feel my phone vibrating like crazy in my bra, but with how tightly my boobs are pushed against Ryker's back and the speed we are going, I don't want to risk losing it to the wind. It will just have to wait until we stop, but I could take a wild guess that the news has gotten out and it's either Remi or Conor checking on me. When I find out who has sold me out to the newspapers they'll find themselves being hung, drawn and quartered.

I can feel the bike starting to slow as we come over a peak in the road. My mouth drops open at the sight before me. The beach goes on for miles upon miles, stunning white sand and blue crashing waves. Now I have seen it, I can smell the salt in the air. I must have been so deep in my thoughts I didn't even notice. The closest beach to London is over ninety minutes away and now that we are here I just want to rip the helmet off and take a deep cleansing breath of fresh air.

I forgot how imposing London can be. I'm lucky I live in a rather green area with loads of trees and plenty of grass. But after spending hours today staring at the bland concrete buildings, the sight of the beach is disbelieving. I hadn't been to the beach in years. Not since Grandad had taken me when I was younger, but that is a whole other story.

Pulling the bike into a dirt car park, he leans it over to one side while kicking the stand out. I can feel his breath coming in deep pants. Slowly I peel my arms from around his waist and try to give him some breathing room. I can feel my crotch pushed right up against his arse. I'm not going to lie, every twist and turn we took, I could feel him clenching his muscles, including his glutes. This may or may not have caused me to rub my clit all over him.

I raise my hands up to unclip the helmet, which surprisingly doesn't smell that bad. All I can smell is his cologne, when I expected it to have more of a musty or sweaty smell. After struggling for a few minutes, I release a huge sigh because it's obviously not coming off. Feeling a slight chuckle vibrating up Ryker's back, I see him turn around, grab my hips and swing me so I'm facing his front. As a result of the quick, unexpected movement, it takes me a few blinks to find my surroundings again. Low and behold, right in front of my face is some yummy pecs covered in a tight t-shirt. The wind from the ride must have plastered the t-shirt to his skin causing it to outline his muscles. Licking my lips, I glance up and see his beaming smile. It's the dimples next to his mouth that makes my mouth water further. How did I not notice them before?

"Do you need a hand?" I hear his husky voice ask. Instead of speaking I just move my head up and down, which causes the helmet to move as well. Oh God, I bet I look like a bobblehead right now. I feel his hands under my chin, his skin feels surprisingly soft for a man, their hands are usually calloused. Once I hear the clips pop, he slowly tugs the helmet off my head and places it on the seat behind him. Quickly raising my hands, I run my fingers through my hair and I dread to think what my helmet hair looks like right now.

Cleaning my throat with a croak, I reply. "Thank you for saving my arse back there. It was lucky you had your bike to hand." I watch as his eyes flit to the sea and back to my face again, the tops of his checks seem to be tinged red. Is he embarrassed about something?

"Yeah, I guess it was," he responds, rubbing the back of his neck. "Want to explain to me why they were coming for you? I highly doubt it's for your speeding ticket." Now it was my turn to be uncomfortable.

"Umm, I'm not really sure." It's not a lie, but it's also not the truth. I truly don't know what story they are hoping to get. I turn my face towards the beach in the hopes of him not seeing the half lie in my eyes. I run my tongue over my bottom lip in the hopes of directing his attention away from my treacherous eyes. I watch as his eyes drop down towards my mouth and see the sexual craving reflected back at me. Subtly arching my back, which forces my boobs higher, I can feel his hands tighten on my hips as a groan leaves his mouth.

Within seconds his hot, needy lips are on mine and I can feel his tongue probing at me to open up for him. When I finally open my mouth his tongue plunges straight in and starts entwining with mine. The need that is crawling up and down my skin causes me to release a moan into his mouth. I scramble on to his lap like a sex-crazed demon, rubbing my needy bundles of nerves against the hardening mound in his jeans. Feeling him grow even harder has me rocking against him. I slide my hands under his t-shirt and run them up and down his chest and pecs. After a few passes I accidentally on purpose catch his nipples with my nails causing him to buck forward.

In a flash he has us off the bike and standing, with about three feet between us. We stand there staring at each other while trying to catch our breaths. Damn, I'm not into dogging, but I would have gone all the way with him on that bike if he hadn't stopped. What the hell came over me? I have never ever been that turned on like that by a guy before. I'm pretty sure that my panties are dripping wet right now. Don't get me wrong, I have had a few sexual partners in the past, but none have made my blood pump like that.

Even just standing here watching him catch his breath has me all hot and bothered. Turning my back to him, I'm now facing the calm sea. Deciding I want to feel the sand between my toes, I bend over and start taking my shoes off. I bent over, keeping my legs straight, making sure he got a nice clear view of my arse. If you have it, flaunt it, right? While still bending over, I turn my head and look at him with a wicked grin on my face and wink. "Last one to the sea is a rotten egg." I've just managed to slip my other shoe off when I finish the sentence and make a dash towards the open water.

"CHEATER," I hear being yelled behind me. Keeping my eyes straight I run as fast as I can, but running in sand is hard. When I'm a couple of feet away from the sea, I notice a shadow approaching fast with thumping steps. Before I know it he has sprinted past me into the crystal blue water. I slow down as I watch him enter the water and run straight back out.

"Fucking hell, that is mother fucking cold. I think my balls have just jumped back inside me to get away from that icicle pop you call a sea." One look at him and I can see he is deadly serious. Before I know it a laugh has creeped up my throat and I'm howling with laughter, like full on bend over howling. I'm laughing so hard it brings tears to my eyes and I struggle to breathe.

Chapter Thirteen

Ryker

I have never seen anything more stunning in all my life, than her standing there laughing her ass off. What a damn fine ass it is too. That show she put on bending over had me so hard I couldn't even think straight. I would have fucked her right there and then on my bike if I hadn't pulled away. There is just something about her, it's like I have been living in a shroud of darkness since my dad's passing and she has come into my life and shined light into it. She has managed to bring the colour back with her carefree attitude.

Having her thighs pushed up against my legs and her pussy resting at my back made it really hard to concentrate. I'm surprised we even made it here in one piece, a few times I lost focus and nearly wiped out. It would be a hell of a way to die, with her wrapped around me. But I would much rather feel her mouth on my dick first. Fuck, I'm hard again. I realise I'm just standing here watching her laugh. Fuck, creeper much. Deciding I need to retaliate, I make my way back towards the water. I'm sure if I kick it hard enough, I can splash her with the freezing cold water. She's laughing so hard she doesn't even see me move. Once in, I slowly bring my leg back in the water and throw it forward as if to kick a ball. I know I have hit my target when I hear an almighty squeal.

"Ahhhhhh, fucking hells bells, that is bloody cold." She turns towards me and I know instantly I'm in deep trouble. I can't help the smile that rises on my face when I look at what I can only assume is her threatening face. This causes me to crack up laughing, just as she had been, bent over at the waist and all. If she thinks that look is scary she needs to come and live in my neighborhood. Before I can stop laughing I feel a sprinkling of water hit me.

This causes me to laugh even harder, if she honestly thinks she can get me wetter than her, with those tiny feet, she has another thing coming. Before I can bring myself back upright from laughing, I hear a war cry and feel her jump on my back. I twist and turn a few different ways, but she is holding on like a spider monkey. Deciding to fight fire with fire, I head back to the sand and throw myself on the ground and roll over. Now she is underneath me, covered in wet sand. I can feel tiny fists hitting my back and shoulders. So I just lay there even longer.

"Is someone there?" I ask with a slight chuckle at the end.

"Off me you great oaf," I hear her voice muffled from behind me.

"Huh, I thought I heard something, guess not." I move my back left and right, just so I can smush her further into the sand.

"Struggling to breathe," I hear from behind me. I quickly jump to my feet, scared I may have hurt her, but she's just laying there smiling. "HA HA, gotcha." Groaning, I take a seat next to her in the sand while looking out at the sea. We both just sit there for a few minutes and let the quietness of the beach wash over us.

"So is Zoe your girlfriend?" she asks while still looking out there, kind of like she is too scared to look at me.

"No, we dated for a little while but now we are just really close friends. She helps me a lot and I help her." Zoe helps me more than I can ever express, but I don't need Isabella knowing that. I don't need to bring my demons to her door step.

"What about that fancy lawyer of yours, is he your boyfriend?" I say while keeping my eyes maintained on the sea.

"Remington?" she asks.

"If that's his name, then yeah, him." All I can think is what a douchebag name that is. Who the hell calls their kid Remington?

"No, Remington III is not now, nor has he ever been my boyfriend. Don't get me wrong, our parents and him would love for us to be dating, and I have thought about it a few times just to get my parents off my back, but I just can't bring myself to do it," she says with a huge sigh. "We have been friends since we were in nappies. But there is only fondness and friendship there for me, I don't feel any spark with him and for me a relationship with no spark is a fate worse than death."

I turn to look at her. "What do you mean your parents want you to date him?" This brings a frown to my face.

"That is a story for another time. I think I need to head back to the city. My phone has been going crazy and it's going to be getting dark soon." She reaches into her bra and takes her phone out. Damn, I was wondering where she was keeping it with no visible pockets. Showing me the front screen, I see she has over one hundred missed calls.

"Fuck a duck, that's a lot of missed calls," I say as she unlocks her phone. I hear her phone dialing a number and then ringing out. A deep voice answers.

Issy, are you ok? I hear in a panicky voice. *Where are you? Are you safe? Do you need me to come and get you?* This is all said even before Isabella has managed to mutter a word.

No calm down, I'm fine, and safe. On the last word she looks me up and down then smiles.

I will be back at the estate in about ninety minutes. Fancy coming and getting me as I have no car?

Yeah, not a problem. See you there. The dude just hangs up, not a bye, not see you soon, nothing. I wonder why she doesn't want me to drop her home, but to take her to the estate instead? I reach into my own pocket and pull out my phone. I see I have a message from Zoe.

Everything is ok here. Some rich guy with a lame arse car came around asking about Isabella, said his name was 3rd something. I didn't give him any information, just told him she had left when the reporters turned up. Picked the girls up from school, they are all sorted.

I responded straight back. *Thanks. Will be home in about ninety minutes, will update you then.* I'm not really a texter and prefer to get straight to the point. Idle chit chat is not my thing and I find it pointless. Rising to my feet, I hold my hand out to help Isabella up.

"Oh a gentleman I see, you weren't so gentlemanly when you were splashing me with water," she says with pointed eyes. She's covered in sand and I can see how wet I actually got her.

"Your chariot awaits ma'am." We have a long drive back to the city. She's wet, sandy and already shivering. "Here take my jacket, you're shivering and it's only going to get colder when we ride back." Sliding my arms out, I hold the jacket out and help her to put it on. Damn, it looks good on her, it reaches her mid thighs. She wraps it around herself as if she is trying to save the heat. If we were still cave people I'm pretty sure I would be yelling and banging my hands on my chest like an ape. Having her wrapped in my jacket with my warmth heating her back up makes me want to own every part of her body. I want to make her mine.

Shit, I can't make her mine. I can't do that to her, I won't force her into my clusterfuck of a life. I should have known fate had her own agenda for us.

When we reach the bike, I lift my leg over the seat as I get the helmets ready. Watching Isabella walk over with my jacket on is doing all kinds of strange things to my body. I want to lay her down on it and fuck her twenty different ways to Monday, but I need to get her home.

She takes the helmet from my hand and slips it on her head. A hush has fallen over us. Being at this beach made it feel like we were living in our own little bubble, but once we look at our phones and remember that there is an outside world which we both have responsibilities in, our bubble seemed to burst.

Raising my hands up, I grab both sides of the under-chin clip on the helmet to fasten it for her. Whilst doing it I gently brush my knuckles against her chin, watching as she closes her eyes. Her skin is so soft and unblemished, the comparison between my hands and hers is startling. When the clip is in place, her eyes reopen. The pain I see in them is heart stopping. Without thinking I move my lips over to place them against hers. I want to take that pain away and bring the light back to her eyes.

I stop before we lose ourselves again in the lust. "Come on, let's get back." Saying those words feels like razor blades coming up my throat. I hate the thought of having to take her back to the estate, so that limp dick, who is slicker'n owl shit, can take her home. He gets to make sure she is safe and taken care of, whereas I get to watch her drive off and then I will most likely spend the rest of the night thinking about her.

Chapter Fourteen

Isabella

I don't want this ride to end, but I can see we are approaching London city again. I grip my thighs tighter around Ryker's muscular thighs, as if any minute I'm going to wake up and this dream is going to be over. What a ride this afternoon has been. Even just thinking about what we did on his bike has me tingling all over and my knickers keep getting damper by the second. I want to run my hands all over his body again. I want to feel his powerful muscles ripple under the strokes of my palms.

As we round the next bend I see the council estate come into view. Its tall concrete structures rise high into the sky. I need to get my armour back in place as I know Remi will be waiting for us there. Hopefully all the paparazzi will have moved on to a better story by now. Knowing them, the vultures that they are, they will be back tomorrow. Fuck, tomorrow. Where will I be doing my community service now? I want to come back here, I enjoyed my time with Zoe and Ryker. Damn, I didn't just enjoy my time with Ryker, it was positively life changing. No one has even made me feel a tenth of what he did.

When the rumbling of the engine stops I know our blissful time has come to an end. Feeling Ryker stiffen under my arms, I can see the cause of the tension in his body when I see Zoe and Remi talking. I don't know if his response is from Remi alone or if it's the fact Remi is talking to Zoe. Grabbing my hand as I lift myself off the bike he uses it to pull me so I'm standing off to the side of him, while he dismouts the bike too. This action causes us to now stand face-to-face. Well actually chest-to-face due to his height. I look up into his eyes, it seems the pain is back in them again. Trying to ease the situation we have found ourselves in, I manage to put my mask back into place and slip into the joking, no-shits given, girl everyone knows me to be. "Thanks for the ride and not just the one on your bike," I say with a smirk, just as

Zoe and Remi reach us.

"You need to call your parents, they are going mental," Remi snaps at me. "Everyone has been out looking for you. The papers have released a story about the Empress of a huge corporation running off pregnant on a motorbike."

"Oh shit!" This is bad, very very bad. My mother will be losing her shit, and I will no doubt get a punishment for that.

"Oh shit, indeed. We have done as much damage control as possible, but you will need to come back here tomorrow and give a statement to the press." Remi is looking at me like I was the one to cause all of this chaos.

"First of all, I want to know who put the call in to the press in the first place." I stare at him with a look that could kill. Remi begins to talk, but my phone goes off at the same time. Slipping it out of my bra I open the message.

Both Remi and I groan at the same time when we look at the same group chat message. Oh fucking hell. What has Conor gone and done now? Another fucking party in my honour no less. I'm going to kill that fucker. Looking over to Zoe, I can see she has crept up behind Remi and is looking over his shoulder at the phone.

"Who the hell are you two? That party is being held in one of the most exclusive nightclubs in

London, and it's in her honour," she says pointing her hand towards me. Looking over at Ryker, I see the confused look in his eyes. I can't take the questions I know he is going to ask. I can see them burning just below the surface. When he finds out who I truly am, everything he thinks about me will change. Turning my back to him before he can voice the questions, I walk away, heading straight for Remi's car.

I just carry on doing what I always do, keep my back straight and my eyes forward. Without looking back I shout, "let's go Remi, we have a party to get ready for." I open the door on his car and slide myself in. It's starting to get dark now as the sun is setting. Taking a deep breath into my lungs, I hold it there while counting to ten in my head before releasing it. It's a coping mechanism I learned years ago. It works when you want to say something and can't, when you want to cry and know you shouldn't. Most of all, it works when you want to scream at the world and know you wouldn't stop screaming until your lungs are stinging and your voice is gone.

A therapist told me to use an elastic band around my wrist and anytime I needed to do something and knew I couldn't, I was to snap the band against my skin. As you can imagine, when I was around my mother for a prolonged period of time I ended up with big welts around my wrists. My mother cancelled those therapy sessions due to, and I quote, 'the therapist making her daughter look like one of these poor people who self harm'. When I went to my dad to protest against it, all he told me was that my mother's words were final. I have never been to him for help again. This is my life and I just have to deal with it.

Lost in a haze of thought I jump out of the car as soon as Remi pulls up outside my house. "You coming tonight?" I ask.

"Yeah, but a bit later than normal, have PR stuff to sort out first." He responds while looking at his phone.

"Alright, catch up with you later then?" I ask. He just nods his head while still looking over his emails.

Slamming the car door shut, I glance over at the huge house. Most of the lights are off, which is a good sign for me, it means the parents are out. Releasing the breath I had been holding, thinking I was about to feel the wrath of my mother, and shaking the fear out of my limbs, I run up the steps and open the front door.

Dashing up to my room I switch on all the lights as I go. I have always found this place creepy as fuck in the dark. It's not at all warm and inviting, it's like walking through a museum. You won't find any pictures of the family on the wall here. More like ugly pictures with old dead people in them that are worth more than my car. They're considered family heirlooms, but like fuck they will be on the walls in my own home. I will just donate them to a much-needed charity or sell them and use the money to build some homeless shelters.

A shower is the first item on my to-do list. I need to remove all the sand from my arse crack. Thinking about how it got there, with Ryker's body on top of mine brings a flush to my face, I can feel my cheeks getting redder with the heat rising to them. I know if I look in the mirror my face will also be adorned with a huge grin. However, the reality is that girls like me don't end up with nice guys like him and that thought crashes down on me like a tidal wave, forcing my shoulders to droop in the defeat of what my life is going to be like.

Fuck it all to hell. I'm going to enjoy it till the bitter end. Time to go drown my sorrows and find a guy to fuck. That's all I'm missing right now, a good old up-against-the-wall fuck. One that leaves marks down your back and has you walking like John Wayne for a few days. Getting into the shower I blast the one song that makes me feel empowered, Love Myself by Hailee Steinfeld. When it gets to the chorus I scream the words as loud as humanly possible.

Scrubbing the sand, and hopefully the feel of Ryker's hands from my body, I feel like I have taken the top layer of skin off. But, I step out of the shower feeling brand spanking new. Striding over to my wardrobe, I rake my fingers over the different types of dresses hung in there. Hmmm tonight I'm going as a badass bitch. I choose a black leather crop top paired with my leather jacket and high waisted, skin-tight, black leather skirt. I run some oil products through my hair and do my makeup dark with almost black eyeshadow and black wing tips adorning my eyes. Finally, I run a dark red lipstick over my plump lips. Okay, I'm ready to go.

Chapter Fifteen

Isabella

Arriving at the club I see Conor waiting outside, leaning up against the valet parking stand. Stepping out of the car I watch his lean body striding towards me, his strapping muscles bulging under his tight black t-shirt with every movement he makes. Maybe he can be my great lay tonight. He's good looking, has a caring personality and is always around when I need him. But can we have meaningless sex without it denting our friendship? I mean, he works for my dad, in the labs. Even though he doesn't have to as his parents are just as loaded as Remi's. When I asked him about it, he said he has always enjoyed chemistry, so I just accepted it and called him a geek.

Would having sex with him just make things awarkard? Maybe we can test it out later. Our relationship has always been open and flirty. We even had that sloppy drunken kiss one night, a long time ago, but maybe now we could go further. Who knows? Perhaps a carefully placed hand on his shoulder, chest or leg will get the meaning across fast enough. I can take him down the hallway to the bathrooms. It's dark and away from the crowd, it will give us a few minutes of privacy.

Conor moves up towards my side, wrapping a hand around my waist and bends down to give me a kiss against my cheek. "Hey baby girl, you look smoking tonight. You on the prowl?" he asks, glancing into my car.

"You know me, always ready for some trouble," I respond with a wink.

"Can I borrow your car for an hour? I will be right back and we can have the last dance," he says, raising the side of his lips to show me his panty dropping smile. It's the twinkle in his eye that always seals the deal.

"Of course, but no more speeding tickets, okay. I'm still doing community service from the last ticket you got," I answer back.

"Scouts honour," he returns while holding up three fingers. Handing over my keys to him, he gives me another kiss on my check before getting into my car. Closing the door he peels out of the car park like his arse is on fire. Taking a deep breath and slipping my mask into place, I head up the steps and into the nightclub.

Once inside I head straight to the bar. Without Conor by my side I don't have a buffer to keep away the parasites. Before I have even managed to reach the wooden bench covered in beer mats, three girls have already stepped in front of me. Oh well, here we go, time to play nice with these fake bitches.

"Hey Isa," Bitch One says in an overly cheerful voice. I look her up and down, starting from her plastic pink heels, all the way to the top of her electric pink hair. I want to give her the number for a better hairdresser as that colour does nothing for her face. Her hair has been straightened within an inch of its life, making the ends of her hair look burnt.

"Hello?" I question back. The way they speak to me is like they know me, but I don't recall meeting them before.

"It's me, Chloe. We were in infant school together, you used to share your toys with me," she counters in a voice full of dismay, as if I shouldn't have forgotten her. I mean she is talking about fifteen years ago and I'm a hundred percent sure she has changed since she was four.

Trying to not start anything with her, I answer back with "cool" while pushing past the two other girls who are just standing watching the interaction. When I reach the bar the bartender is already waiting for me to order. "Screwdriver please," I ask while handing my card over. "Can you open a tab too?" He nods back acknowledging my request.

"Was that you talking to Conor Becks?" Bitch Two asks. Crap, I thought I had dodged that bullet, but here they stand again. Looking over at her I know that the only way I'm going to get these leeches away from me is by applying my bitch persona. When you have grown up in my world you learn fast who you can and can't trust. My ex-best friend sold the story of me losing my virginity to the tabloids for money. If I'd known at the time that her parents had cut her off, I would have given her the money myself. However, she thought it was better to go behind my back and break my trust instead.

"No, it wasn't," I respond back using my most clipped voice while narrowing my eyes.

Obviously not getting the hint, Bitch One counters my statement. "Yes it was, you gave him your car keys."

Picking up my glass, I gulp down the cocktail in one go. Wiping my mouth with the back of my hand, I know I don't look very lady like right now but I couldnt give a flying fuck. I wave at the bartender signalling for another.

Turning back to Bitch One, I'm about to rip into her, but in a way I'll be doing her a favour. They can pine all they want over Conor, but all he will give them is a quick fuck. It's what he's best at, then he will drop them like a bag of shit on fire. I have watched him do it more times than I can count. It's how I know he will be a good choice for tonight. "Look, Conor only screws. He does down and dirty, in alleyways, corridors, and toilet stalls. You girls deserve better. Now please just fuck off. I've had a really long day and I just want to drink, then have a quick shag, preferably finishing with a mind blowing orgasm."

Once my speech is over I see that the bartender has left me another glass full of orange juice with vodka. Picking it up, I decided to make my way to the dance floor. Taking a sip I smile to myself, maybe I will fuck the bartender. He knows how to make my drinks, with more vodka and less orange juice. Once I reach the dance floor I start swinging my hips around and adding in some slut drops.

After a few songs, covered in sweat with an empty glass, I make my way back to the bar. I take a sneaky look around and see that the three bitches are no longer standing anywhere near it. Knowing that my coast is clear, I head straight over. Placing the glass on the counter top, I see the bartender making his way towards me.

"Another?" he asks.

"No thank you, too much orange juice will give you the shits," I respond, causing the guy to bend over laughing.

"What caused him to lose his shit?" Remi asks next to me. Where the hell had he come from?

"The truth about orange juice," I answer back while still looking over at the bartender. "Can you get me a bottle of 1996 Dom Perignon Rose Gold Methuselah?" The bartender looks back and forth between us and I glance over at Remi, a little bit confused as to why the waiter is looking at us like that.

"Um, we have one bottle, but it costs thirty seven thousand pounds," he says, still bouncing his eyes back and forth.

"Okay," I respond slowly, not fully understanding the issue here. "The card I gave you has a high limit, so it will go through," I look over to Remi again, he has his hand over his mouth and is trying to stop the laugh that is dying to break out. Moving my eyes back to the bar, I watch as the bartender speed walks over to his manager, says something in his ear and points towards us.

Recognition lights up the manager's eyes, suddenly the man is springing into action sending the bartender in the other direction as he strides over to us. "Miss Jonson, thank you for gracing our club again. Tim has just gone to retrieve the bottle for you. He should be back shortly, would you like for us to keep it on ice for you."

"Yes, thank you. If you could take it over to the VIP section for me that would be perfect," I respond with my overly cheerful voice.

Turning around I make my way over to the private VIP area. It has plush red couches covered in suede, low lighting and a heavy thick curtain. However, I know for a fact each booth is monitored with a camera. The best part being your very own dedicated waitress. Stories have been told about what the waitresses are willing to do for money behind said curtain, but my boat has never pointed in that direction. I'm a lover of the dick.

Our waitress heads over with the ice bucket, glasses and bottle of champagne. She looks over at Remi who is sitting on the couch with his arms spread over the back, looking as relaxed as ever, which is strange as this isn't normally his cup of tea.

"I will be your waitress this evening, my name is

Cindy. Just push the bell if you need anything and I'll be right over," she says as if butter wouldn't melt. It's overly sickening and the hair toss at the end has me rolling my eyes.

"Oh God, I think I just threw up in my mouth," I say voicing my thoughts. Cindy turns her eyes towards me. I can see fire burning in them as it seems she doesn't like that I've just called her on her shit. Suddenly remembering who she is firing daggers at, the fire dims fast. As if fate is on my side this evening, Gold Digger by Kanye West starts to pump out of the speakers. Laughter bubbles up inside me and before I know it, it's exploding out. Raising my hand up to cover my mouth, trying to stop the laughter, I look over at Remi and can see he is trying to stop himself from laughing too.

Cindy turns on her heel and storms out past the VIP section like the devil is licking at her heels, causing me to laugh even harder. That song was so perfectly timed even Lucifer himself couldn't have done it better. Grabbing the clean champagne glass that has been left next to the ice bucket I fill it up to the brim. Part of me just wants to drink it straight from the bottle, but as much as my mother would disagree, I do have some class. Lifting the glass up to my lips, I take a large sip. The bubbles tickle my tongue and the sweet taste coats my mouth. I know the minute the alcohol hits my system as the dark cloud that seems to be hanging over my head starts to dissipate. If there's one guarantee in my life it's that champagne can make me feel all light and fuzzy.

The club looks a little on the empty side tonight. Opening my phone, I bring up Instagram and snap a picture of Remi's sour face and mine. God he's never liked having his picture taken and no matter how relaxed he looked before, his face instantly sours when he sees it's picture time. I think from all the time we have spent together, I only have one actual picture of him smiling and it was one I managed to take candidly when he wasn't watching. When I showed him, he wanted me to delete it, but I point-blank refused.

The photo turns out dark, but I'm definitely keeping it. Popping a caption in, I then tag our location. I would bet my car that this place will be heaving within the hour. With all the people who want to be part of our click.

We sit in comfortable silence for a little while, both of us lost in our own thoughts. Just watching the different people bump and grind on the dance floor. The overwhelming urge to join them shoots through my body. Standing up sharply, I grab my drink and finish the glass before heading over to the dance floor. Looks like Conor isn't coming back anytime soon, so I'll just find someone else to scratch my itch. After a few unknown songs have played, still no one has come over to dance with me. Looking around I see that Remi is standing by the red VIP rope.

Seeing that Remi is watching me, I walk over to a random guy and start rubbing my tits up and down his back. When he turns around and sees who is dancing with him, his eyes shoot over to Remi's and then he is suddenly walking off the dance floor. I point at Remi, that fucker has been cock blocking me.

"This is bullshit," I shout as loud as possible, causing a few people to turn and look at me. Well that has just royally pissed me off. The next song comes on and I know this one. It's Buttons by The Pussycat Dolls, which means it's time to get my stripper on. After gyrating through the first few beats of the song and a well placed slut drop, I feel a body push up against my back. The smoky smell I would know a mile away, guess Conor is back then. If there is one person Remi won't mess with it's Conor. I feel like putting my middle finger up at Remi, but I think that may be a bit too childish even for me. Instead, I just flow with the music and enjoy the growing boner I can feel against my back. I feel his breath pass my ear as he whispers, "Damn, you are so fucking sexy tonight Issy."

Glancing over at the VIP section, I see that Remi is no longer standing there. This is my chance. Grabbing Conor's hand, I lead him off the dance floor and down the dark corridor, out of sight of everyone. Placing my back against the wall, I grab his t-shirt and pull him down towards me. Slamming my lips on his, I move my tongue over them asking for permission to enter. I can still hear the music playing in the club and Turn Me On by Riton & Oliver Heldens starts playing. Holy fuck, it's like the DJ is inside my head tonight.

Our tongues start fighting for dominance as I slide my hands under his t-shirt and upwards to his pecs. When I finally reach his erect nipples I pinch them, forcing him to buck against me and groan around our kiss. Breaking the kiss he says, "You know I only fuck Issy, is that what you want?"

"Fuck yes, that is all I want, like right now," I rasp in between breathy pants. Once the words are out of my mouth he is grabbing my hips, lifting me up and jamming his hips in between my thighs. With my back still touching the wall, I grab his hair with both hands and bring his lips back to mine. I can feel his dick standing to full attention and straining to come out.

Moving one of my hands down, I head towards his zipper. His hand slips up the inside of my thigh underneath my leather skirt. One of his fingers rubs at my silk panties, which are no doubt drenched. He slowly starts to move his finger around my clit over the top of my thong, all my muscles bunch together preparing for the release I know I will find.

Lost in the haze of lust that Conor has me in with

his mouth and finger, I don't see the mass come barreling towards us. Next thing I know I'm sliding down the wall and Conor is on the floor with a guy on top of him. The guy is straddling Conor's waist with a fist held high, ready to pound it into his face.

Chapter 16

Chapter Sixteen

Ryker

Zoe and I arrive at the club that Remi had given her the address for, I don't know why we are here, it looks well out of our price range. Without breaking her stride Zoe walks up towards the bouncer, who seems to be in charge of letting people in. After giving us a look over and deeming us unworthy of this place he shakes his head. Well, we should have known better, they don't let our kind into a swanky place like this.

Zoe gets her phone straight out and her fingers are flying over the screen as soon as the guy dismisses us. Within seconds of her shooting off the text, I see her look up to the door, and a huge smile graced her lips. Remington the 3rd, King Douche Canoe himself is making his way towards the bouncer. When the bouncer spots him he quickly unclips the rope and a few cameras flash behind me. I can hear them shouting out for Isabella, asking Remi where she is. Zoe never said she would be here tonight, but I probably should have guessed. With my feet moving of their own accord I forcefully shoulder bump the bouncer on the way past, making his apologies now that he knows who our so-called friend is. King Douche Canoe is leading us inside the club and over to the VIP section. I quickly roam my eyes around trying to spot her mass of pink hair. When I finally spot her she's holding the hand of a guy while heading towards the back of the club. Before I can stop myself I'm striding past the VIP section and trying to follow.

As I get around the corner I see red. He has her pushed up against the wall with her legs around his waist and his hand up her skirt, doing God knows what. I start barreling towards them, all logical thought leaving my mind. Upon impact I feel the guy fall to the ground and I'm on him in an instant. I have this overwhelming need to plunge my fist into his face over and over again. My chest is heaving up and down with my panting breaths. Doesn't this fucker know she is better than this. She deserves more. She deserves the sun and the moon together.

"What the fuck is your deal?" I hear her screams from behind me and feel her hand touch my back, I move my eyes to look over at her. She is pacing back and forth in the small corridor. Rising to my feet, with the fucker on the floor quickly forgotten about, I take in her outfit. From the leather crop top, which shows off her perfect stomach, to the leather mini shirt. She is a fucking wet dream walking. Her hair is all over the place, probably from that fucker running his hands through it. I want, no, I need it to be my hands.

"What the fuck is my deal?" I say seething. "What the fuck is my deal?" I repeat walking closer. "You are my fucking deal" I scream at her. How the fuck can she ask me that. We had an amazing time at the beach today. She was the first person I have ever really connected with and had fun with since my father's death.

"I'm not yours or anyone else's. I just wish everyone would leave me the fuck alone. All I wanted was a quick mind blowing fuck to take my mind away for a split second," she is screaming back in my face now. "I just want a moment of happiness, of pure fucking bliss. I want to be just a nameless face being fucked in a hallway."

"Well why the fuck didn't you just ask?" I suggest while taking her further down the corridor. I look over and see that the dead man, who had his hands all over her, is no longer on the floor. We are completely alone and I'm glad.

Pressing her up against a secluded wall I place my leg between her thighs, I can feel her wetness soaking into my jeans. I grab the sides of her head with both of my hands and bring it closer to mine. "I can make you forget," I whisper against her lips, I don't know if she can hear me over the pounding bass of Fuck Away The Pain by Divide The Day. The irony of the song isn't lost on me. "Do you want me to make you forget?" I say right next to her ear. A small nod from her head is all the answer I need. "Hold on darling, this is going to be hard, fast and dirty."

Planting my lips against hers, I suck her bottom lip between my teeth and bite down on it. She groans into my mouth and I can taste copper on my tongue. Using my hands I rub them over the erect peaks of her nipples, which I can feel through her leather top. Grabbing her hips as hard as I can I shove her against the wall and force her legs around my hips. A warm feeling spreads through me, knowing that tomorrow when she looks at her naked body she will see my fingerprints, no other fuckers, just mine. The thought of her seeing my mark on her makes my dick swell inside my pants. But this little session isn't about me, it's about her. Her and her alone.

Keeping her pinned to the wall with my body, I

rip the little bit of silk that is covering her pussy away, quickly sliding the panties into my back pocket. She lets out a whimper as the cold air from the corridor hits her right in the promised land. Taking my fingers I rub them over her lips collecting the moisture and spreading it across her overly sensitive clit. Her hips jut forward begging for penetration. Knowing she is wet enough to take it, I slide down the zipper on the front of my jeans, and use my balls to cup my boxers under. I thrust my dick straight into her. The force sends her head back against the wall and a deep moan comes from between her parted lips.

She is so damn tight, I can feel her muscles clamping all around me. I start pumping in and out of her before she has fully become ready for me. Pinching her nipples between my fingers I give them a twist, I know just how to give her pain which borders on pleasure. By the look on her face she's loving it.

Oh God, her walls are so tight around my shaft, I don't think I'm going to last long. Slamming into her a few more times I feel her explode around me. While she rides out her orgasm I feel her nails drag down my back, no doubt leaving her mark too. As her hands reach the bottom of my back I explode into her. Once my dick stops twitching I slide out of her and pull my boxers and pants back up, buttoning them before I turn and walk away.

Once I get to the end of the corridor that leads back onto the dance floor, I spot Zoe in the VIP section talking to Remi. Making my way over to the table I pick up a beer that looks like it is sitting waiting for me there. I can't imagine any of these rich dudes drinking beer. They look more like whiskey drinkers to me. I nod my head in Zoe's direction, as no doubt it was her that got this drink for me. She looks behind me and I can feel Isabella is standing behind me, but she walks straight past me. Isabella grabs the champagne bottle from the ice bucket and drinks directly from it. Wow, she is damn classy, I think to myself sarcastically. I keep my eyes locked on her, she is a complete enigma. I never expected her to be a completely different person than the girl at the beach.

A guy and a girl pop out from behind a curtain one booth over and stand next to Isabella.

"Cindy, your name is Cindy right?" Isabella asks with scorn in her voice.

"Yes, what can I help you with?" she says with an overly sweet voice. I think her voice just gave me cavities.

"I would like a few rounds of shots since we are celebrating tonight. So 20 shots of Jager please." All of this is said with her eyes locked on the guy. I think it's the guy who had her up against the wall earlier, but it was dark so I'm not 100% sure. But by the way she is throwing daggers at him, I would bet money on it.

"Oh how rude of me, I haven't introduced you all," Isabella says. "Conor, this is Ryker, who just hate fucked me down the corridor. Ryker, this is Conor, he is the guy you knocked to the floor for trying to get into my panties." Raising the bottle of champagne to her lips she takes a huge swig. Not being able to look at me, she walks straight past me and heads for the dance floor. Watching her walk away, I feel guilt slam into me. I hate myself for what I have just done. How can she see what we just did as a hate fuck?

Fuck, how could I do this? I should only take what she gives me. I can't drag her into my life, it will only end up dirtying her shining soul. She doesn't belong in my world, just like I don't belong in hers. Glancing over at Zoe I can see the sadness in her eyes for me, like she knows what I'm thinking. I need some fresh air.

Chapter 17

Chapter Seventeen

Isabella

God, I hate myself right now. Don't get me wrong, that was the best sex I've had in ages, but it felt dirty. After he just left me standing there, with his cum dripping down my legs, I felt rejected and alone. All I wanted to do tonight was lose myself for a few hours. Is that so much to ask for?

Clutching the bottle of champagne to my chest, I swing my hips back and forth to Turn Me On by Kevin Lyttle, letting the music flow through me.

I watch as trampy Cindy walks back to the table with a tray loaded with shots. Rushing back over I pick one up from the tray and slam it straight down. The burning sensation slides down my throat and makes my body shiver, but the slight warming sensation in my stomach helps.

Grabbing another one, I rise it up toward Remi and Conor and slam that one back too. Looking over at Zoe I'm taken aback by how not drunk she looks. "Come on girl, don't leave me hanging. You can't watch me drink all these by myself, you have to help!"

"I'm down for that. We only have crappy community service tomorrow anyway, maybe if we drink enough we can both still be drunk tomorrow." This is all said with a shot held high in between her fingers. "To community service," she yells and I follow suit. Taking yet another shot down in one gulp.

I grab Zoe's hand and yank her out to the dance floor shouting, "It's my jam bitch," while My Humps by The Black Eyed Peas blasts from the speakers. We dance for what feels like forever. Sometimes we dance with each other, other times with strangers. Stumbling back to the VIP section I see that Remi is sitting talking to Ryker. They look to be having a serious conversation as they are both using hand signals to explain, and the more they talk, the more the hand signals become animated.

Deciding that tonight should be about fun and not anything serious, I make my way over to the table on wobbly legs. Thinking that it's most likely the shoes that are causing me to tilt and sway I try to take them off without face planting the ground. By the time I get to the table both men have their eyes on me. I look between them and decide I need to make an announcement, but my tongue just doesn't seem to want to work. Maybe if I show them what I'm trying to say. Lifting one foot onto the table and then the next, I stand on the table before them. It's at this point my brain decides that my jam is playing and tries to complete a series of stripper moves. Now, maybe if I hadn't been intoxicated I could've pulled it off, but not while I have a bottle of jäger and champagne mixing together in my stomach.

Did it just start getting hot in here? I look around to see if anyone else seems to be getting as hot as me, but Zoe is still on the dance floor. Remi and Ryker just seem to be transfixed on me. Starting to feel like I'm about to overheat, I reach up and start to unzip the back of my crop top causing both guys to jump into action.

"Ok, time to get you home!" Remi declares while keeping my arms pinned to my side.

Rolling my eyes, I slur out, "Nooo- More drinks... more dance." It's hot and I'm starting to feel woozy, maybe if I just rest my head on Remi's chest for a few minutes I will get my second wind. After closing my eyes I can feel my legs give out from under me and the smell of ocean and diesel wash over my senses. With the gentle rocking motion I can't fight the sleep that is taking over me.

"Don't worry, I have her," a husky voice murmurs just before my eyes see black.

Waking up to the feeling that a badger has been shitting in my mouth was definitely not on my agenda for today. Shit on a stick, I feel like absolute death right now. I can feel the room spinning, even though I'm laid down. My mouth starts to fill with saliva, which can mean only one thing, I'm going to puke. Jumping up and running on unsteady legs, I dash to the bathroom before the contents of my stomach ends up all over the floor. Kneeling on the bathroom floor and praying to the porcelain Gods is how Remi finds me.

"Wow, you're not looking so good Issy," he says with a smug grin etching his face and a twinkle in his eye. I can tell he is enjoying this moment a little too much, he's revelling in my pain.

"Gahhhh," is all I manage to get out past my lips without the need to throw up again. Remi is nice enough to pass me a glass of water and my tooth-brush with toothpaste already squirted on it. I brush my teeth while still sitting on the floor, using the toilet to spit into.

"I don't think I've seen you this bad in ages, care to explain?" He says in his 'I know more than you' voice. It's the voice he uses when he's trying to prove a point, or when he thinks I'm being stupid. A bit like the time I made him take me to a tattoo parlour to get my first tattoo. I'm still proud of the little elephant I have on my hip bone. It's grey with a sugar skull face, shaded in using my favourite colours pink and teal. I even had him put a little bow on its head, right between the ears. I love it, the details are amazing with swirls in black all throughout. Remi walks over to the shower and starts pressing the different buttons. Like I said before, he will make an amazing husband one day, just not mine.

Using the toilet to stand up, I hold on till I know my legs are strong enough to keep me upright. "Ten minutes is all you have, so be quick about it. There's a cup of tea and some pain killers waiting outside for when you finish," he says while striding from the bathroom and leaving me to shower.

Anytime I try to bring up memories from the night before, I come up blank. I remember getting to the club, getting some drinks, meeting Remi and heading to the VIP lounge, but after that it's blank. There is nothing after that, not even snippets of memory, just blackness. I'm assuming if Remi is here to pick me up then my car is still at the club. I will have to get it later. My brain hurts too much to even think about things like that right now. Today is going to be one of those one step at a time kinda days. If I make it through the day without puking again or face planting, I will consider it a win.

Stripping off the old concert t-shirt and panties I have on, I wonder how I got home, no doubt I have Remi to thank for that and changing my clothes. Looking down I notice bruises maring my hips. Huh? I think to myself. I don't remember getting those. They are a deep colour of purple and look like fingerprints. Counting ten of them I'm positive they are fingerprints. Come to think of it, I do have the feeling of sex between my legs. It's like a pleasant aching sensation. But who did I have sex with? I remember waiting for Conor to come back to the club, so maybe it was him?

Jumping in the shower I know I don't have much time to get ready, but I need to wash away the disgusting Isabella from last night and this morning. I have another day of community service to get through. I wonder if they will deduct the hours spent at the beach, as I was technically run out of the estate by the different news outlets. My brain is so fuzzy I don't even have the mental capacity to calculate how many hours I have left. Maybe I should just take the time in prison, at least then I'll be away from this life.

Finishing up in the shower I walk out of my bathroom with my head hanging low to find my mother and Remi standing talking. This is really not what I need this morning.

"Good morning Isabella." She stands there dressed in a white Gucci fitted dress, with brass buttons in a line down the front. Her hair is scraped back into a tight bun with not a single strand out of place. Her face already has a ton of make-up on and it's not even nine in the morning yet.

"Morning Mother," I respond without even looking in her direction and heading straight toward my clothes. I hear her follow me inside the walk-in wardrobe and close the doors behind her. Oh fuck. I take in a huge breath of air and release it slowly. Hoping that I can magically disappear into a black void, I close my eyes, away from the wrath I feel is heading my way.

"How dare you disrespect this family," her voice comes out quiet and close, so close I would say she is standing directly behind me. Grabbing my hair, she spins me around so I'm facing her. "Do you have any idea what people are now saying about you?" No, I really don't think I do. I think she may have to be more specific. I know the club brought in a rule a few years ago about taking photos inside, after another rich elitist got caught out in a cheating scandal from photos taken inside the club. I know some of the press have tried to encourage some of the lower elitists to take pictures for them, but the threat of a lifetime ban from the most famous club in London is enough to deter anyone.

"Don't ignore me when I'm talking to you, bitch." She grabs the top of my arms and brings my face closer to hers. She is gripping my arms so tightly that I'm going to have bruises to match my thighs.

"I'm, I'm, I'm..." I stammer, before taking a deep breath. "I'm sorry, I wasn't ignoring you, I was just wondering what I should wear today so I don't disappoint the family." I try looking down at the floor, knowing it will only make her more angry if I look directly at her. She says it shows a lack of respect.

"Nothing can undo the pictures of you riding off on a motorbike with a druggy who looks like he belongs in prison. I'm surprised he didn't kidnap you and hold you for ransom. Do you have any idea what Remi and I went through trying to find you?" She takes one hand away from my arm and grabs my chin, her nails digging into my skin. I'm going to end up with half moon indents on my face if she carries on. "Today the press shall be there at the beginning of your shift for you to give a statement that Remi has written out for you. You will recite it word for word. Do you understand me?" My eyes have started to water from the force she is using and the pain she is causing with her grip on my face.

"Yes Mother, I understand," I reply in a whisper. SLAP. The sound of skin hitting skin rebounds around the tiny room. The sting on my face hurts like a motherfucker and I can feel my cheek already starting to redden with an outline of her hand print. It's still not the worst she had done to me. The time when she broke my arm and just left me broken and in pain was one of the worst. I had to call Remi to take me to the hospital and we were only ten, but I knew I couldn't ask my own driver to take me. He would have been on strict instructions not to take me anyway, for fear of people discovering the truth.

Without looking up I can tell she has left the room. Sliding down the shelves, I sit in a pile on the floor. Only then do I let the tears flow from my eyes. I sense Remi before I see him as he enters my closet. He bends down and wraps me in his arms while I release all the pent up anger and frustration I feel towards that horrible woman. I don't understand how I could have grown inside her, before coming out of her body, and yet be so different from her.

After all my tears are dried up I feel a small semblance of normal. Maybe I'm lucky enough to have just cried the last of the alcohol out of my system. Remi helps me to my feet and asks me with his eyes if I'm ok. He learnt a long time ago not to actually ask me. I nod back and give him a little smile in return. I grab some black leggings and a long white shirt, this should be fine to wear for my press release this morning. Not sure how it will survive washing graffiti off the walls though. Lastly I grabbed a pair of red ballet flats. They are the only pop of colour I have. My own tiny way to rebel.

Leaving the wardrobe, I take a seat in front of my vanity mirror. I hate having my hair tied back but I know it's what my mother wants. Grabbing the hair brush, I run it through the long strands before grabbing my hair with both hands and twisting, ready to pin it into a tight bun. Looking at myself I hate what I see. My eyes look all puffy and swollen, my skin looks pale and my cheeks sunken into my face. I have red marks maring my skin that will need to be covered with concealer. Everything all together makes me look ill and not my usual bright self. I imagine this is how I will look everyday if I take on the life my parents want me to.

Chapter Eighteen

Isabella

Arriving at the estate, I can see a wooden podium already erected in front of rows of seats that are full of people from the press. I've always hated this. When I was younger and Dad would have to give speeches, I would be forced to stand there holding my Mother's hand and smiling. I always wondered if I smiled hard enough would my face crack? But that never happened, maybe if it had I wouldn't have to do them anymore.

"You know what to say. Just stand up there and

get the words out then walk off, that's all you have to do. You are not obligated to answer any of their questions," Remi says while taking my hand in his. Nodding my head back at him, I have spent the whole ride here memorising what was written for me. Taking a deep breath, I school my features, place the rod along my spine like I have been taught, and open the car door.

Stepping out I know I have a face that my mother would be proud of. Following Remi to the podium I let him open up the speech and introduce me. I've never understood the need to introduce the speaker as everyone here already knows who is going to be giving the speech or they wouldn't be here in the first place. Stepping up to the podium thousands of lights start flashing before my eyes. Waiting till the light show in front of my eyes stops and I'm able to see again, I stand proud. The worst part is that my mother has managed to turn one of the best afternoons of my life into a shit show. Right now, my afternoon with Ryker feels dirty, it feels like I shouldn't have gotten on the back of his motorbike. I don't know how I'm going to face him and Zoe now after all this.

"Good morning, ladies and gentlemen. Thank you for being here today." Come on Issy you can do this, I say, mentally give myself a pep talk. Deep breaths, in through the mouth and out through the nose. "I have come here today to clarify my actions from yesterday. I'm not pregnant as the tabloids would have you believe. I climbed on the back of the motorbike yesterday as any sane person would do when they have several people running towards them, with flashing cameras and microphones." Deep breath, just keep breathing. "I'm here participating in a community outreach program to help clean up OUR estates, the ones the governments are leaving in such a state of despair. This community is a hazard to children and the elderly. We need to help rebuild them, to make them a safe zone again, and with the help of my father's company Jonson & Jonson, who have graciously donated new equipment and the materials needed to improve this area, we will do just that. Thank you."

Finishing my speech I bow my head in shame, the dirty lies just roll off my tongue but leave an ashy taste behind. Remi walks up to the podium and takes my hand then leads me away. Like always he is holding a bottle of water ready for me to drink. With the hangover, the crying, and now this, I'm sure my body will be hitting dehydration soon. Feeling a body approach my back, I tense thinking it may be Ryker because we left things kind of awkward after the beach. I need him to stay away from me. He brings all sorts of warm and fuzzy feelings inside of me, and I can't drag him down my rabbit hole. We wouldn't survive, he wouldn't survive. Turning on bitch mode I school my features and turn around towards him.

"Who pissed in your corn flakes this morning?" the stranger says. Who the hell is this guy? He isn't the guy I was expecting. Looking him over, I can see it definitely isn't Ryker. This strange looking guy doesn't hold a candle to Ryker. Giving him a once over, I see that he is wearing a burberry cap paired with a blue polo top and white Nike track-suit bottoms. He has more gold chains around his neck than Mr-T and the gold rings on his fingers are huge and gaudy. In fact, he reminds me of the crab in Moana. God, what was his name again? I'm going to have to Google it once this creep is gone.

"Do I know you?" I ask with as much distaste as I can. The guy seems to take this as an open invitation and steps closer, invading my personal space. I look behind me at Remi to see if he will step in, but he seems to be on the phone talking animatedly to someone. I would bet my inheritance it's my mother. I hope his dad's company is charging my mother extra for all the PA work Remi is putting in.

"No, but as head of the welcoming committee for the estate I thought I should come over and introduce myself," he responds with a sneer, causing a shiver to run down my spine.

"OK, so introduce yourself?" I say questionly. Then I will know what name to give to the police to put on my blacklist.

"The name's Dave," he answers with a smirk and a wink. Nasty, this guy is like a greasy slimeball. I can't stand guys that think they are God's gift to humanity. He's nothing like Ryker, who doesn't seem to know how fit and sexy he is. "If you need anything, just hit me up, and I mean anything." I can feel his eyes raking up and down my body, and I watch his tongue come out and lick his bottom lip. I smile back at Dave, while the song Fuck You by Lily Allen streams inside my head.

"Of course Dave, I will keep your offer in mind," I reply, keeping my shudders to a minimum. Turning around so he knows this conversation is over, I see that Zoe's talking to Remi and standing next to her is Ryker. Just looking at him standing there with faded ripped jeans, t-shirt, and leather jacket, has me drooling. Even his Doc Martens look amazing on him. I want to run over and wrap my arms around him, plant kisses all over his sun kissed face, and dance into the sunset with him, but my brain holds me back. I can't bring my darkness into his life. He has already been through so much with his dad dying, I won't drag him down more. I refuse to be the reason that his soul is blackened any further.

Lifting his eyes to mine, I see a spark of lust light up his eyes, but it's quickly chased away with embarrassment and then anger. In an instant he is taking long strides towards me, his body locked up in anger. Fuck, is he coming for me? I'm stuck to the floor like a statue, unable to move away from his empowering force. But I see his eyes are no longer on mine and are instead pointed directly behind me. Turning my head around I see Dave is still standing behind me. Fucking idiot, did the prick not get my memo when I turned away and stopped talking to him.

As soon as Ryker reaches us, he places himself in between Dave and I. "Ryker, Bro. How are you this fine morning?" Dave's eyes are alight with mischief. I'm not sure why, but I get the feeling these two know each other. Ryker takes another step toward the slimeball just as Remi and Zoe reach us.

"Issy, you ready for some fun." I hear Zoe say behind me with a chipper voice. Damn, does that girl wake up with the sun coming out of her arse? Slinging her arm around me she steers me toward our community service advisor. Guess my time is up, and the start of another day fulfilling community service begins.

Turning around while walking backwards I yell over to Remi, "Remi, I forgot a pack lunch again, can you grab me something? I promise to pay you back in kindness." I say with my sweetest voice and puppy dog eyes. He can never say no to that.

"I will make sure you have something for lunch. Would hate for you to get any skinnier, or we could lose you down a crack." This has always been his go to response when I used to tell him my mother had me on another diet or she had told me I was looking fatter.

Grabbing both boobs I yell back, "I have no chance of getting lost down a crack with these." This causes all three guys to start choking. Looking at Zoe I see she has that look on her face, like she wants to ask me a question.

"Just say it," I say to her. I like it when people can be honest with me and just tell me whatever is on their minds.

"Say what?" She sounds confused.

"Just ask whatever question is plaguing that brain of yours, it's written all over your face."

"Are you and Remi... fucking... or have you guys ever fucked?" she responds while looking embarrassed.

This question causes me to break out with belly clenching laughter. I find myself laughing so hard tears come to my eyes. "Nope, we have just been best friends for a very long time and he is the only person in the world I trust. Plus, Remi doesnt fuck, he dates and makes love," I say honestly, when I'm able to curb the laughter.

"Huh?" She sounds confused. We arrive at where the community support manager is standing with our buckets of water and sponges. People have

never understood mine and Remi's relationship,
but I've never given a shit about it.

Chapter Nineteen

Ryker

Dave, that slippery eel fucker. I should've known that after the dog and pony show this morning with Isabella, he would've found a way to speak to her. Seeing her standing there talking to him has my blood boiling. I want to storm over to them and slam my first into his smirking face.

I could see her up on that podium, her face a blank slate, but her eyes screamed out in pain. Zoe stopped me from walking over and standing next to her. I was desperate to hold her hand and give her strength. I don't know what it is about her, just something makes me want to protect her. But after last night and what I did to her, I wouldn't be surprised if she never wants to see or speak to me again. I've asked Zoe to do some recon for me, I'm too chicken shit to do it myself. I need to find out what she remembers and find out how high I am on her shit list. I know I can't have anything with her, but I also can't stand the thought of her hating me.

When she asked Remi about lunch I could see that he was torn, muttering under his breath about meetings and not being a personal lapdog. So I jumped in to offer to sort it out for him, but of course the slippery eel also heard. I'm hoping he doesn't plan on making an appearance, I'm not sure how many times I can stop myself from smacking him in the face. He knows too much about me, things he could tell Isabella. Pissed at that thought, I head back to the flat so that I can count down the hours until lunch.

After sorting the flat out, putting all the toys away and cleaning up the kitchen, I head over to the window and watch Zoe and Isabella are working on the same wall as yesterday. They seem to be laughing and joking around, all the tension from this morning has left Isabella's body. Thinking about her body has me growing hard in my pants. Remembering the way she moved that body on the dance floor, the way it felt sliding into her while having her thighs wrapped around me, her breath panting in my ear with every thrust I made, just gets me hotter.

Slamming noises coming from in the kitchen brings me out of my lust induced thoughts. Looks like mom is awake. Oh joy.

"Ryker!" she shouts. "Where is the fucking coffee?" I hear over her slamming cupboards and drawers. She carries on cursing till she finds the right cupboard, the same cupboard the coffee has been in since I moved here and cleaned out all the expired and moldy food. "What the fuck is the point in you living in my flat if you're not here to help?"

Walking over to the kitchen and leaning against the door frame, I watch her fumble about in her come down stage. It's the same thing every morning. At first I used to yell at her and she used to yell back, but I've learnt to just keep my mouth shut. If I don't, the girls will end up paying for it later. I know that all I have to do is stand here, and let her take her frustration out on me instead.

She walks her grotty ass over to the couch after grabbing a spoon and her rubber tourniquet off the table where she dumped it before. Pulling a plastic bag from her pocket, she carefully pours the powder onto the spoon. With a flick of her lighter she proceeds to melt it down and suck it into an already used needle. Getting HIV has never been a concern of hers, the high is worth the risk.

Wrapping the rubber tourniquet around her arm, she feels about with her fingers trying to find a vein. She has injected into them so many times before that they are mostly damaged, but I see what I think is her version of a smile when she finally finds one. Once the crap is injected into her vein, I watch as her whole demeanor changes. Within minutes, her shaking has stopped and she falls back against the couch. Her eyes roll back and a look of euphoria passes over her face. She'll spend the rest of the day in her bedroom off her face. Guys will come over to get high with her and fuck their brains out. They won't be here long, walking out after leaving money on the table. Money that will further her drug addiction. Not buy new clothes for her kids, or food or even basic necessities. She has only one care in the world and that is getting high.

My dad had always been honest with me regarding her addiction. He'd never sugar coated it or lied to me. Even from a young age, I knew my mother was alive and a drug addict. But being so far away it had never affected us. We got on with our lives and she got on with hers. I'm not here to look after her ass. I couldn't care less if she died. She has never cared about me, so why should I care about her. I'm here to look after my two half sisters who I never knew I had. I only found out about them at my dad's last will and testament reading. Apparently, even though they were not his children he had still been sending my mother money to look after them. I knew I had to come over to take care of them. They are my sisters after all. I couldn't allow them to fall into the same life as my mother, I want more for them.

America held nothing for me anymore, so after selling everything I climbed on a flight and came here. When I found the shit hole they had been raised in, I was shocked. When I knocked on the door I was greeted by two little girls who were in clothes that didn't fit, covered in dirt, and playing with used needles. Since that day, I have been the one to take care of them; feed them, dress them, and send them to school everyday. They are all I have left in the world, and I'm all they have. They mean everything to me, and more.

Glancing over at the clock I see that it is approaching lunch time. Heading to the kitchen I start opening and closing the cupboards looking for something to make for Issy. Shit, I didn't think this through. What happens is she is allergic to something, and ends up in hospital. Nope, stop over thinking this. She ate lunch yesterday when you made it. Whipping together a picnic that would make the queen proud, I go back over to the window. Glancing down I see they are packing up ready for lunch. Grabbing the carrier bag with the food in, I all but sprint down the stairs, I want to beat slippery Dave to them.

When I break out of the stairwell I spot him straight away, fucking shithead. He has Isabella backed up against a wall with his hand above her head. She seems to be looking around for help, but Zoe won't start anything with Dave for fear he will take it out on her family. But Dave needs me, it's how I know my sisters will always be protected from anything. Our mutual agreement means no one will lay a finger on them or deal drugs to them, while I work for him that is.

Striding over, I see the moment Isabella knows she is safe. Her eyes hit mine and I sent a reassuring smile her way.

"Did Dave not bring you lovely ladies some food?" I ask when I finally reach their sides. Dave turns his head in my direction, but keeps his arm locked above Isabella.

"I was just telling the girls here about a house party tonight on the estate, over on Finch Street," he responds with a snarl at me, like I'm interrupting something personal.

"Why don't you let the girls eat, I bet they are tired from all the scrubbing they have been doing," I say as calmly as I can manage. If he doesnt move that arm soon, I may just break it. This overwhelming need to protect Issy is a new sensation for me. I've never been this way about girls before. My family yes, but not a girl I barely know. Maybe it's from all the guilt I'm feeling about last night. I shouldn't have let last night go as far as it did, but with how she was she was dressed and how she was acting. My basic need just took over.

Shoving my body in between Dave and Issy causes Dave to stumble back several steps. He can see the possessiveness in my eyes, but just smiles at it. Grabbing Issy's arm I walk over to the other wall and slide down it so my ass is on the floor. Giving her arm a quick tug, she lowers herself to sit next to me. The brush of her arm against mine causes goosebumps to break out along my skin. Opening up the bag which has all the picnic food in, I place my hand inside and pull out two sandwiches handing one to Issy and one to Zoe.

"What no sandwich for me?" questions Dave in a joking manner.

"No." I respond sharply, "I obviously didn't get that memo."

"Well, girls to do, people to see," responds Dave while turning and walking away. Before he reaches the double doors to enter the building he turns back around, yelling to me over the park. "Don't forget our arrangement for tomorrow night." With that the wanker walks inside the building.

"Yuck, that guy gives me the serious creeps. I wouldn't be nice to him if he didn't own the whole estate, but you saw what happened to the last family that got on his wrong side," Zoe responds with a shudder. Seeing the confused look on Issy's face I fill in the missing blanks for her.

"They were beaten to a bloody pulp before they were run off the estate," I say this while looking at the floor. Feeling her stiffen beside me has me looking up into her eyes, they are the size of sourcers. "If I can give you one bit of advice Issy, it's to stay the hell away from him." I hope she can see the truth of that statement in my eyes because I have a feeling that Dave will try his very best to get closer to Issy, as he can see that she is from money.

Chapter Twenty

Isabella

Getting to the party, I can see that it is already in full swing, cars are parked left right and center. Booking an Uber was definitely a better decision than calling Remi. He would see the pain in my eyes, he would know from the way I was carrying my body what had gone down at the dinner table with my parents. Even now, I can still hear my father's voice loud and clear, as if he was still yelling it at me.

"I own you! You will do as I say." Spittal was flying from his mouth as he etched these words into my brain. Glancing over, I could see my mother and the glee she was getting from this conversation. "You will come and work at MY company, like MY daughter is supposed to. We have been patient with you long enough. We have let you play your games and enjoy your life. But starting Monday you will be at the company and you will work for ME." He stands with such a force that his chair went flying back from the speed in which he stood up. I have never seen my dad this mad before. He's never raised his voice to me, other than that time I went to him about mum.

Grabbing my face hard, he looks me dead in the eye. "You will forget all this stupid nonsense about going to university. You will work at my company, you will marry into a wealthy family with a nice son and you will produce an heir for me to pass MY empire on to. DO YOU HEAR ME?"

"Yes Father." At my agreement, he releases my face and I take this opportunity to run from the room and straight out the door. Getting my phone out of my bra whilst walking down the long drive, I ordered an Uber. I knew this day would come, I've always known. They were never going to let me live my life the way I want to. They have always been grooming me to take my place in the family business. I just can't believe one speeding ticket has caused all this. A speeding ticket I didn't even get. If I had known it would come to this, I would have told the courts I wasn't driving. I would have kept my head down.

When the Uber finally arrives, I hop in and give the driver the address to the house party the creepy guy told me about earlier. "Miss, are you sure you want to go here, this address is in a nasty part of London?" the stranger says.

"Yes, I'm sure. Can we stop at a petal station on the way, I'm feeling a little thirsty?" Little does he know, I'm not thirsty for water. What my dad said tonight is playing on repeat in my mind, like he has just signed my death warrant. Pulling into the first petrol station we come across, I jump out of the car and head inside. Picking up a bottle of Jack Daniels I head over to the checkout to pay. I'm glad the price is under £30 so I can use my phone to pay, as I ran out of the house so fast I forgot my purse.

Heading back over to the car, clutching my life-line like it can help with all the despair flowing through my body, I slide into the vehicle and open the bottle. Taking a big gulp, I can feel the burning of the whiskey as it flows down to warm up my tummy. For the rest of the journey, I sit drinking and watching London pass by outside the window.

As I look around at the housing estate I've been brought to, I can see lots of people spilling out of the house. My happy buzz gives me the courage to walk up to the door and strut inside despite not knowing anyone here. The moment I step inside the door I hear, "The Princess has arrived," before slippery Dave is throwing an arm over my shoulders. "And she came bearing booze." Dave shouts with spittal flying everywhere. I raise the half empty bottle up and give everyone my award winning smile. Maybe if I'm lucky enough I can drink myself into a coma tonight and never have to step foot inside his company, and by his I mean my father's.

The bass is blasting and everyone seems to be dancing, so I join them. I stand on top of someone's coffee table, gripping my bottle and swaying my hips. Then the need to pee hits me full force. I have been putting off popping my cherry, as everyone knows once you break that seal you will spend the rest of the night peeing. But I can no longer resist. Stumbling off the table, I fall into slippery Dave's arms, I swear that guy seems to be stalking me. I yell into his ear over the music, "Toilet?" He raises his arm in the direction of the bathroom. I decide to salute him for answering my question. Heading into the bathroom to sort out my business, after flushing I look into the mirror. The person looking back at me isn't someone I recognise. She looks like a stranger. I have bags under my eyes, they are bloodshot and my hair looks limp and straggly. This isn't how I went down to dinner, I was dressed up, looking my best. That is the only way you can have dinner with my parents. They like to believe every family dinner is like a gala event.

I don't notice the door open or close till I see wet slate eyes looking directly at mine in the mirror. When did Ryker get to the party? The eyes have me transfixed. It's like they can look through everything and see the pain I try to bury deep. He can see all my flaws, all my scars and all my imperfections. I feel like nothing with his piercing gaze, he is able to strip away all my bullshit and leave me bare. No one else is truly able to see past my armor, but he does. I need to break the tension in here before it suffocates me. "Do you often follow girls into bathrooms?" I sass.

"What the hell are you doing here? I told you not to come." The venom in which he says these words towards me, hits like daggers. But all it does is just piss me off. What is it with men, thinking they can just demand things from me and I'm going to fall into line. I'm my own person! When will these shitheads learn? Will there ever be a time a man isn't trying to boss me around?

"Who the fuck do you think you are? I can go where I like, when I like," I snap back whilst trying to budge past him. He grabs me to stop me passing and pulls my back against his front. Then he pushes hard into my back, showing me how I make him feel. I can feel his cock straining against his jeans. Little does he know, he has the same effect on me. Looking back up into the mirror, I'm taken back by the lust I see in his eyes and it's all for me.

I push my arse into his boner, making my intentions clear. Taking one of his hands off the counter he runs it up the back of my leg. When he reaches my underwear, I see a fire flash in his eyes at my wetness.

His husky voice, his own personal smell, everything about him turns me on. Using his hips, he pins me against the counter. One hand runs up and down the seam of my underwear, while the others trails softly up my arms and slips the strap on my dress down my arm. The way he is caressing my skin brings a shiver and causes goosebumps to break out all over my body. With the back of his hand, he runs it over my already peaked nipple causing a moan to escape my mouth and my eyes to close.

"Open your eyes, and watch me love your body," he whispers into my ear causing my eyes to open in a flash. Pushing my dress further down my body, he watches as both of my boobs pop out. Spinning me around so I'm facing his body, he takes one of my nipples into his mouth. His hot breath against my already cold nipple makes it peak even harder. Not wanting the other nipple to feel left out, he pulls and twists it, causing beautiful pain. My hips buck forward and I throw my head back thrusting my boobs further into his face.

Taking my hand, I reach down and slowly run it over the steam on his jeans. It must be painful being that hard while being that confined. Popping the button on his jeans and pushing them past his hips, allows his dick to spring free. Using the pad of my thumb, I run the bead of pre-cum around his tip. A guttural moan passes his lips causing more goosebumps to rise up over my skin.

When Ryker grabs both my hips, I let out a pained gasp. His fingers are right over the bruises from the sex I has last night. I don't even want to think about last night right now. Reaching over I grab the bottle of JD I must have left on the counter while I was peeing. Pressing the rim to my lips, I open up and feel the burning liquid travel down to my belly.

I tentatively allow my eyes to drift upwards and find Ryker is glaring at my hips with a look of what I think might be shame. Maybe he is embarrassed to be in here with me. With that sobering thought, I start to pull up my dress and try to pass by him.

"Issy?" he asked confused. I feel so dirty, he deserves someone better than me. He deserves someone who is his alone. Hell the last thing I remember from last night is dragging Conor off the dance floor so we could fuck and now I'm about to fuck him. My skin feels like it's crawling with the realisation of him thinking I'm a slut, if he ever found out. As drunk as I am, I'm not drunk enough to do that to him.

Seeing the pity in my eyes has him reaching out

for my arms to comfort me. When his fingers wrap around the top of my arm, I accidently release a painful cry. He grabbed me in the same spot my mother had this morning.

A look of anger crosses his face. "What the hell issy, are you in pain?" he asks. While trying to look in my eyes. "Why does the top of your arm hurt? I didn't hurt that part of you last night." Confusion clouds my mind.

What the hell is he on about, last night? "Huh, what about last night?" I'm so confused and my brain just can't seem to compute right now. Drinking down more of the amber liquid, I'm hoping it may help clear up the confusion some more. Because alcohol can help with that, right? NOT!

"I asked you a question, answer me!" he all but shouts at me. I raise up to my full height. I'm sick to the back teeth of people thinking they can demand things from me. That they can talk to me like shit. Treat me like they fucking own me. Nobody owns me. I'm shaking from the anger coursing through my body right now.

"Don't fucking talk to me like that, you don't know me," I seeth back to him. "I don't have to explain shit to you."

You would think I had just hit him with the way he reacts, his head rears back. Within a blink the shock has passed and he returns to staring back at me. Using his arms he cages me to the counter. His eyes flicker back and forth between my eyes, like he is trying to find the answers to the universe in them. The only thing he will find in my eyes, is a lost soul. Turning my head away from him, as I can't take the staring contest any longer. He pushes his lips gently onto mine and uses one hand to run down my arm, over where the bruise is.

Confusion crosses his face as he rubs his thumb and fingers together. He obviously doesn't understand the concept of concealer. "What is all over your arm?" he asks while still looking at his fingers.

"It's concealer, like what girls wear on their faces to cover spots and marks," I whisper back. He hasn't reached the point of understanding yet, but it's only a matter of time until he does.

"Why would you wear concealer on your arm?" he says while trying to inspect it. Maybe I can drag this out as long as possible and fate will bestow me by having someone come into the bathroom. This would give me a chance to escape without having this conversation. Yeah fucking right, when has fate ever been on my side. I'm positive fate is in bed with my mother sometimes.

"To cover marks?" I say with a patronising tone. I'm in self-defense mode and being a bitch, so I say it to make him feel stupid and hopefully he will drop the topic. Huffing out a breath, I can see he is losing patience with me.

Chapter Twenty One

Ryker

I. Am. Seething. How the hell does she have bruises on her arm? I know she is trying to play stupid so she doesn't have to explain herself. If I find out she had sex with someone else last night I will explode. I know we are not exclusive, but still. If she still had not been satisfied after our first round, I would have happily taken care of her. I would willingly take care of any itch she has. I will take care of her, till her forever comes.

Taking a deep breath, I try again. "Why are you trying to cover marks on your arm? More to the point, what marks are you trying to cover?" Waiting for a response, I know I'm not going to get anything because all she does is raise her shoulder in a shrug sort of way. Fine, guess I will have to find out myself. Grabbing the nearby hand towel, I run it under some water then dampen it down. Slowly and as gently as possible, I move the towel over her skin. I see the concealer come away and in its place is a black and purple band around her arm, maring her perfect flesh.

The shock must flash on my face, as she shrinks back from me. These are not marks from sex or even angry sex. These are marks from abuse. Who the hell is abusing her like this? I'm going to kill the motherfucker. If I find out it's Remi, I don't care how Zoe feels about him, he is a fucking dead man. Zoe think's I don't know that she likes that douche canoe, but I'm not stupid. She never stops fucking talking about him and I've never seen her get that girly look that she has when he's around. But if he is the one hurting Issy, I won't let him anywhere near Zoe to hurt her too.

Trying to unclench my teeth and allow words to pass my lips feels like a near impossible task right now. Taking some calming breaths, I can feel my heart rate slowly descend back into its normal beating pattern. "Who did this to you?" I ask. Her eyes are shooting around the room, landing on everything but me. She looks like a caged animal getting ready to fight or flight. Without trying to make the bruise worse, I gently run my fingers over it. I need to calm her down and find out more about this.

Keeping my voice gentle I ask, "was it Remington who did this? I can protect you from him, I can help you." She let out an angry laugh, which I wasn't expecting. "Was this his punishment for you sleeping with me last night?" I try and ask in a soothing voice.

"What?" she asks while looking at me directly, her eyebrows are pulled with one side of her mouth tipped down. "We had sex last night?" Fuck, she doesn't remember. Zoe did say that Issy had no recollection of us being there last night, but I just thought that maybe she hadn't wanted to discuss the fact we had sex. But I can see from the way her eyes are shooting back and forwards, as if trying to find any type of memory in the deep recess of her brain, that she genuinely cannot remember our first time together

"Oh God, I *am* a slut," she whispers to herself while taking her head in her hands. Wow, that hurts. Just because I'm not from her neighbourhood she considers herself a slut for sleeping with me. Fuck, why am I even here? She could have just knifed me and I would be in less pain.

"You're acting like I'm riddled with diseases!" I snapped at her, her words have definitely caused my ego to take a hit.

Issy looks completely stunned by my comment. "No, I don't mean it like that." She looks at the floor with embarrassment. "I had sex with you and Conor last night," she whipsers. Her body seems to collapse into itself and she wraps her arms around her body for support.

What? When the hell did she have sex with this Conor guy? It couldn't have been after we had sex as she was too passed out. It could have been before. Wait, isnt Conor the name of the guy I pushed off of her?

"Conor? As in the guy I knocked off of you in the corridor?" I ask whilst thinking back on that devastating moment. I'm sure that was the guy's name. I stopped it. She didn't have sex with Conor, but if I hadn't have got there when I did, I'm sure she would have.

I'm one hundred percent sure she didn't have sex with Conor before us. Voicing this out loud to her, I can see she is confused by the way her eyebrows are drawn together over her eyes. So I help by filling in the blanks for the missing time she has blacked out. "When I arrived at the club last night you and Conor had just walked off the dance floor and were heading down the back corridor. When I finally managed to get to you his hands were up your skirt." Admitting this has my hands balling into fists. "I pushed him to the floor and was about to start punching him when I felt your hand on my back." Taking a deep breath, I know I need to get these next words out, but it will not be easy.

"I was so angry at seeing another man touch, caress and kiss you the way I wanted to. I wanted it to be my tongue sucking on your nipple. I wanted it to be my finger running through your folds, and most importantly I wanted it to be my dick buried balls deep in you," I admit to her. I can see that my words have the desired effect when her pupils become almost black with full blown lust. "I know that we can't be together, but I will take any morsel of you that you're willing to throw my way." Saying that last part has me glancing at the floor with embarrassment as I feel I have just shared my soul with her.

She closes the distance between us by bringing her lips and placing them against mine in a gentle caress. I can feel the pounding music and conversation on the other side of the bathroom door, but right now it feels like me and Issy are caught in our own little bubble. Opening my mouth to her, I give up the control and let her plunge her tongue inside. I will give her all the control she wants and needs if it means I get to see her smile.

Using my hands I run them up and down her sides, slowly grazing the sides of her boobs with each pass. I must accidentally hit a ticklish spot as a small chuckle escapes her parted lips. Her laugh is the sexiest thing I've ever heard. Looking deep into her eyes, I can see lust shining back at me and a small grin raises the side of my lips. In the next instant she is grabbing my head and forcefully pulling it back towards her. Tilting my head to one side she runs her tongue from my collarbone up towards my ear, while taking little nips at my skin as she goes. My dick is about ready to jump out of my pants. Not being able to hold off any longer, I gently tweak her nipples causing her hips to thrust forward.

Removing her hands from my hair, she runs them down to my chest and to the hem of my t-shirt. Me giving her a small nod of encouragement to remove it is all she needs. Once the material has been removed from my body a small gasp leaves her lips. I don't have very many visible tattoos, but underneath my clothes is a different story. I have covered most of my skin and it has become almost a memento of my past life. Her fingers start at the skull just above my right pectoral muscle and she follows the vine of roses down to the waistband of my jeans. Each of the four roses represents someone special in my life, but lately I've been thinking about adding a fifth rose.

While she's inspecting the rest of my body I slowly slide the straps down on the diamante body con dress she's wearing, I release a little gasp still shocked from finding the lack of bra, even though I knew it was coming. Like a starved man I devour her nipple like it's the last meal I'll ever eat. Grabbing her hips, I lift the dress up and see that she is also going commando. A groan is released from my lips as I know this woman will be the death of me. With my hands on her hips I lift her up onto the counter and press myself between her legs. Using the growing bulge in my pants, I rub my denim covered cock against her core, causing her to release a long guttural moan.

With swift fingers she pops the button on my jeans, releasing my straining cock. Using her soft hand, she grabs it at the base and runs it up the length of my shaft. Her hand feels like velvet gliding up and down. I'm transfixed watching it happen. I can feel the skin around my balls tightening, it's embarrassing to say, but at this rate I'm not going to last long.

Grabbing the top of her hand to stop her pumping motion, I move it back to the counter and instruct her to grip the edge. I want to get her off first before I spill my load. Taking a finger I run it up and down her wet folds and with my thumb I begin circling her clit. I know when I've hit the spot as her hips buck and a moan is released from her lips.

"Get ready Sweetheart, I'm about to bang you like a screen door in a hurricane," I purr in her ear just before I thrust inside her slick, wet core. Her hips arch towards me, letting me slink in deeper. She feels like soft velvet and oh so tight. Lifting herself higher, she manages to sink her teeth into my shoulder while I pound into her. The pleasure and borderline pain combo has my dick growing thicker inside of her, my balls getting tighter, ready to release its seed. I know only a few more pumps into her and I will be blowing my load, but I want her to come at the same time as me.

Reaching between our bodies, I run my hand down her neck, between the valley of her perfect tits, past her belly button and around her clit. Just as I'm about to apply the pressure to the magic button I bring my teeth down to bite her nipple. The pain with pleasure causes her body to respond as I expected. Her inner muscles tighten, her eyes roll back and a scream leaves her lips. Watching her gorgeous climax is too much for me, I quickly follow her climax with one of my own. My body shudders and I explode with a growl.

Placing my head on her shoulder, both our chests are rising and falling in rapid breaths. This here, this right here, is bliss. I wish we could stay like this forever, in our own little bubble. Before I can get any words out, my phone starts blasting it's obnoxious ringtone from my jeans pocket. Reluctantly I slide out of her warm core and bend down to grab the phone. I am really hoping it isn't one of my sisters calling with an emergency.

Chapter Twenty Two

Isabella

Ryker holds his phone up towards his face and releases a long sigh. That's not something you want to hear from the guy who just had his penis balls deep inside of you and you're still trying to clean yourself up, whilst coming back down from cloud nine. That was one soul shattering organism. I don't think I will ever, in my whole life, find another man who can do that to me. I'm scared to even get down from the countertop as I don't know if my legs will hold me up. They still feel like jelly.

"I'm sorry, I have to go and deal with something," he says while still glancing at his phone. "I won't be long, please just stay in this bathroom," he pleads whilst looking deep into my eyes, which only emphasises the impact of him leaving me in here. "This party is dangerous. Lock the door and wait for me to come back. Only open the door for me, can you do that?" By now, he is back in my face looking at my lips. Suddenly my lips are feeling very dry and my mouth parched. His eyes follow my tongue as it darts out to moisten my chapped lips.

"Sure," I responded, while inspecting my nails. It's easier than him seeing the hurt in my eyes. My answer seems to bring him out of the haze he has been in since picking up the phone. He seems torn between leaving me here, and going. Watching him have an internal argument with himself is funny. His head keeps swinging to the bathroom door and back to me again. Taking a deep breath, he kisses me on the forehead and heads to the door, with his mind made up.

"I promise I will be back in two mintues, then I'm taking you to get some food. Consider it a date," he says while winking at me and closing the door. Despite his talk of taking me on a date, I'm suddenly feeling all alone in this bathroom and very exposed. Looking around for a washcloth or a towel, anything really to clean myself up with would be handy. But now the buzz from the alcohol is wearing off, I can see how much of a dump this place actually is. Looking around for my bottle of JD, I'm desperate for a drink, my tongue has started to stick to the top of my mouth. Plus, I don't really want to be drinking the tap water here. Well the water itself isn't an issue, just the amount of dirt around the tap itself. A shiver passes over my body at the thought of drinking from there.

Spotting the bottle on the floor I reach down and pick it up. "Damn it," I say out loud. The bottle is empty. "Sorry Ryker," I say to an empty room, "but I really need to get a drink."

I need to scope out the situation and so I walk over to the door, open it a little and pop my head out. The hallway is packed with people. That's good, I can get lost in the crowd. Closing the door once again, I head back over to the mirror for one last check to make sure my dress is in place and nothing is hanging out, like a nipple or something. My parents would love that all over the front pages of the newspapers tomorrow morning at breakfast time. I could see in my mind the coffee spraying out of my mother's mouth and it flying across the table. Which I would also get the blame for might I add.

With everything put away and in its place, including my nipples, I head to the door and open it wide. Striding out of the bathroom, I'm on a mission to find a drink, while internally saying, "nothing to see here people". Nope, I didn't just get royally fucked in the bathroom. Who the fuck am I kidding, these people most likely heard the scream that came out of my mouth. They probably heard me chanting Rykers' name like he's a God.

Heading into the kitchen, as surely this is where people would keep their drinks, I see bottles and cups and crushed cans lying on every surface possible. I spot the spirits in the sink, filled with water in an attempt to keep them cool. Glancing around I see no cups anywhere. Guess the bottle will do. As I unscrew the cap and press the bottle to my lips, I feel the liquid burn a path down my throat. It's at that point someone decides to grab my arse. Swinging around, I can feel fire lighting my eyes at the intrusion of privacy. I see a man standing there with a leery grin and several missing teeth.

"Hey girly, you drink from that bottle like I want a woman drinking from my cock," he slurs at me.

"Nasty! Look, but don't touch what you can't afford," I spit back at him.

"Oh you're one of those high end hookers? Dave, really went all out tonight," he says while getting in my personal space and running a greasy hand down my arm.

"Please don't touch me, I'm not a prostitute." I respond while moving out of his reach, keeping the vodka bottle clutched against my chest. He reaches to grab me, but I manage to slip past him and run into another room. The crowd seems to swallow me up and takes the disgusting man out of sight. Walking away and releasing a huge breath I didn't realise I was holding, I managed to find another door that leads to a garden. Before I can walk through the door however, familiar voices reach my ears. Crouching down to try not to be seen, I creep forward and can see Ryker and Conor standing in front of each other.

Before I have a chance to say anything to them and let them know where I am, Conor thrusts a large brown package into Rykers' waiting hands.

"Does Issy know you are dealing drugs?" Conor asks Ryker with a sneer in his voice and a look of savageness on his face that I haven't seen before.

"Does Isabella know you are using her father's company to make the drugs, Conor?" Ryker snarls back at Conor, with a look of disgust.

At this proclamation my head starts spinning. What the actual fuck? I have heard enough. My legs start to move, but I have no idea where I'm heading as my mind is running a mile a second. People try and stop me by grabbing my arms, but I'm too numb to feel anything except the ringing sensation in my ears.

I manage to run straight through the house and out into the street, not dropping the bottle of vodka along the way is a miracle in itself. I don't stop there, I just keep running. After a while, my breath comes in short pants and I know I'm far enough away from the house. I let the tears escape and slow to a walk. I feel so fucking stupid. I feel so damn used. Conor is one of my best friends, but not only is he making and dealing drugs behind my back, he is using my Father's company to do it. That must be why the fucker is always using my car. I bet he was on his way to deal some drugs when he got that fucking speeding ticket.

That damn speeding ticket that has ruined my life. The stupid ticket that caused me to go to court. The mornic ticket that has me doing community service. That crackbrained ticket that has caused my parents to lash out and force me into a job I'm going to hate. But most of all that fucking ticket that brought me to Ryker, who has now caused my heart to break into millions of pieces. What a fucking dick! Just like everyone else, he was using me for what I can give him.

My brain starts to wander towards Ryker, his betrayal hurts worse than anything. He has broken the last bit of my heart that was left to give. I so badly wanted things to be different with him. I had hoped that no matter my parents or my life, we could've had something real together. That day at the beach was the first time I didn't have to wear a mask with anyone. I was just myself. He's now taken one of the best moments in my sad existence and crushed it into nothing. Just some sand to blow away in the breeze. Maybe that's why he wanted to get close to me, so I could get him a job at a father's company and he could then compete with Conor. My imagination is spiralling, thinking up all the possible reasons for his betrayal.

Thoughts come and go through my head as I walk down the street drinking from the bottle of Vodka I still have clutched in my hand. Maybe I should just go and marry Remi, at least I know he wouldn't hurt me like this. I could have a happy life with him, right? Well maybe not happy, more like boring. But at least it wouldn't be as soul crushing as this. Maybe I should call him? My feet start to stumble all over the pathway. Or at least I think I'm walking on a pathway.

Taking the phone out that has been squished between my boobs, I call the only person who I can trust. He answers on the first ring like I knew he would.

"Issy are you okay? Where are you?" Remi says panicking through the phone. "Just tell me where you are and I will come and get you," he continues.

"Remi, I'm sorry I could never be the person to

make you happy," I respond as if I haven't heard his questions. My mind is somewhere else right now.

"What are you on about Issy? Just tell me where you are so I can come get you." I can hear some commotion behind him. It sounds like someone is trying to get the phone.

"Issy, baby, please tell me where you are. What happened? I asked you to stay in the bathroom so you wouldn't get hurt. This place is dangerous and people will try and hurt you," Ryker responds in a shaky voice.

"Just leave me alone. Go back to dealing drugs with Conor. You hurt me! You have hurt me enough for everyone around here. You cut me open! You left me bleeding!" I shout at him through the phone, trembling with rage. Before I know what I'm doing, I throw my phone into the bushes lining the path. Not my smartest move, but I'm hardly at my best right now.

Chapter Twenty Three

Ryker

"**F**uckkkkkkkkkk," I internally scream. She must've seen me and Conor outside in the back garden. I can't fucking believe this. Remi is looking at me like I'm a piece of shit. Well I guess he would be right.

After finishing with Conor, and giving the drugs to Dave, I headed straight back to the bathroom and found that she was gone. After asking a few people about her, they said she ran out of the house with a bottle of vodka and tears streaming down her face. Straight away I called Zoe to get Remi. If anyone knew her, it was him. He arrived at the party twenty minutes later. Right now, we are all standing on the front lawn trying to find Issy. By we, I mean; Remi, Conor, Zoe and I. We fucking look like damn Mystery Inc. Two preppy dressed guys standing next to Zoe and I. Normally, we both look like homeless people next to them in their designer suits and expensives watches, but around here they're the ones that stand out, and Zoe and I are in our element. Zoe grew up on these streets, she knows them like the back of her hand. If anyone can find Issy on the estate, it's her.

"Does someone want to fill me in here? What the hell was Isabella talking about? Why does she think that you two were dealing drugs?" Remi demands. I can see why he makes a good lawyer now. He looks formidable.

Conor raises his arm to rub the back of his neck, he seems to be looking a bit hot under the collar since Isabella's declaration. "I don't know man, maybe someone spiked her drink and she is tripping," he responds bashfully. "Man, you know how these sketchy ass, dump house parties can get," he mumbles while pleading with his eyes, silently asking me not to say anything.

"Bullshit, that is exactly what she saw." I shout at him. "You know full well what she is talking about. I can't believe I never put the pieces together till tonight. I had this strange feeling last night in the club that I'd seen you somewhere before, and now I know!" Zoe walks over to me and places her hand on my arm. I look down and can see in her eyes, Issy being missing is causing her to suffer just as much as it is me. "You have been dealing with Dave for years, I've seen you on several runs." Looking towards Remi I ask, "Does Issy own a Aston Martin Vanquish in light blue?" I say with raised eyebrows, "as that is the car he," I point at Conor, "always arrives in."

Remi looks over at me and then at Conor. "You have been using Issy's car for drug runs and then having her take the blame for your speeding tickets?" he roars, stalking towards Conor. "What the fuck is wrong with you?" He raises his arm and swings it at Conor's face, punching him dead in the nose. A cracking noise echoes around the air and blood starts gushing out of his nose and down his face. Dripping all over his white pressed shirt. Remi steps away from him curling and uncurling his fist. The shocked look on Remi's face means this is probably the first time he's punched someone, but with the way his pupils are dilating, I'd bet my life on the fact that he enjoyed it.

"Dude! Was there any need for that?" Conor muffles while trying to cup his nose and pinch the bridge at the same time to stop the blood flow. "I think you broke it, my nose is going to be all wonky now," he whines. "Girls dont like guys with crooked noses," he groans while walking away and reaching for his phone.

"What would've happened to her if they had taken her car and found your fucking drugs in them? Well let me tell you, she would have gone to jail because of you." Remi takes a deep breath, I can see that he is shaking with anger and getting ready to lash out at him again. Instead, he turns his anger towards me.

"I expect this behaviour from that sack of shit. I've always known he's fucking shady, but you, all your police checks have come back clean." He huffs out a frustrated sigh. I can't believe he actually ran a background check on me!

"I honestly hoped she had a future with you. For years she has been taking abuse from her parents and from society, she's been used and abused by everyone she has ever known. I wanted you to be the person to change all that for her. I could see from the way she looked at you after you went to the beach. You lit a light inside her soul that had been dimmed a long time ago. Her shoulders were sagging less, like a weight had been lifted," he says while shaking his head, "but you are no better than him," he deflates while rubbing a hand across his forehead.

"Don't you dare say that to him!" Zoe angrily responds to Remi while poking her finger at his chest. If the situation wasn't so dire it would be funny. Zoe, with her little body, trying to intimidate Remi who is twice her size. "You don't know what it's like living how we have to. He does this to protect his family. You have no idea what he has been through after arriving here. How dare you judge someone who is trying to make the best of a shitty situation. You get to sit in your ivory tower throwing money at everyone who questions you, never having to get your hands dirty. You know nothing." By the end of her rant, her chest is heaving as she tries to take in huge lungfuls of air. Zoe will always defend me, she has seen my ups and downs. She has seen the fights between me and my mother's clients when they have looked at my sisters. She has seen the tears I have let escape in my moments of weakness. She's been my one true friend here, standing by me and always being there to help me. Plus the chick just quoted Games of Thrones in a rant, that makes her a badass in my book.

"None of this blame game is helping us find her? Can you track her phone or something?" I ask with a small bit of hope. Even if I can't make amends with her, or get her to understand why I have to do it, I still just want to make sure she is safe. I will happily watch her from afar, if it means her light still shines. I couldn't stand the idea of me being the person to dim her light again.

Looking over at Remi, I have a sudden need to ask a question. "Tonight she had bruises up her arms, are they from her parents?" Remi glances at

Conor before turning back towards me. He slowly nods his head up and down, I can see the pain in his eyes for her. I don't want to ask for any details now while Conor is standing right here, that fuckard doesnt need to know anymore about Issy. The dickhead is still standing off to the side grumbling over his 'ruined good looks'. He already has my blood boiling over. If I hadn't watched Remi sucker punch him, I sure as hell would have.

I can see now that the relationship Remi has with Isabella is not a romantic one, it's one of friendship built up over many years and lots of crappy situations. The relationship he has with Isabella is no different than the one I have with Zoe.

Looking over at Zoe, she is my only hope right now of finding Isabella, since Remi says her phone can't be tracked. "Zoe, you know the area better than any of us here, where do we start?" I look at her, hoping she holds the answers we all need.

"Ok, if I was a drunk Issy with my life crashing down around me, which way would I go?" she mumbles to herself, while looking around.

Chapter Twenty Four

Isabella

When my feet decide it's time to stop, I glance around at my surroundings. Huh! I seem to have been stumbling down an old train track and have stopped on a bridge. My foggy brain decides it wants to see how high up we are. Walking over to the wooden ledge and peering over, I see we must be a few hundred feet above a river. It seems deep but not fast moving, probably from the lack of rain we had all summer.

Picking a stone off the floor, I want to see how

long it takes to reach the water. Releasing it from my fingertips, I count; one Mississippi, two Mississippi, three Mississippi, splash. Hmm not as far down as it would seem, but I guess the darkness can make it seem further away. Climbing up onto the wooden railing, I swing my legs up so they dangle over towards the river. I bet this has an amazing view in the daytime, but tonight the waxing crescent moon doesn't provide enough light to see far.

All the bramble bushes around the train line makes it obvious that it's no longer used, but it does have a worn down path in the middle, so joggers and dog walkers probably use it during the day time. You know, when they can actually see where they are walking. I wish I'd been allowed a dog or a pet growing up, maybe it wouldn't have been so lonely. Then I would've had someone to actually talk to. Someone who isn't paid to listen to my crap, but actually wants to listen to what I have to say.

When I was a child, I had all these amazing dreams about becoming a famous scientist and finding new cures for different things. I was going to take over daddy's business and lead it down a better path. When the nannies used to let Remi and I play together, we would pretend that Remi was a world class doctor and I was a world class scientist. Together we would make the world a better place. I would create the cure and he would administer it. Remi may not have become a doctor but he has his career and from what I've seen, a budding romance with Zoe. I don't want to ruin that for him, he could achieve so much more with his life if he didn't have to constantly babysit me. Plus, Zoe's going to get tired of him always coming to my rescue. Maybe everyone would be better if I wasn't here.

Hell my parents wouldn't even miss me. Remi would, but he would soon get over it. I thought Conor would have, but after what I've seen tonight I know I'm just a means to an end for him and Ryker. It's the last person on the list that brings tears to my eyes. I can feel the water drops running down my face. My parents would never let anything happen between us, they would end up locking me in the basement before they let me date that riffraff.

The thought of never again seeing his grey eyes sparking, or smelling his personal scent of leather and diesel, brings a small sob from my lips. No, I'm doing the right thing. My world would only rob the sparkle out of his eyes, he would eventually hate me. I know what I have to do. I have to relieve everyone of the burden that I am to them. With shaking legs, I bring myself up to my full height when standing on the railing. Up here it feels so freeing. My pastel pink hair is being pushed off my face with the gentle wind. It reminds me of the beach trip Ryker and I took on the back of his motorcycle. It felt so freeing, kind of like this moment in time. Turning around so my back is to the view, I take a deep breath to fill my lungs and give me courage. With my arms stretched out beside me, I release all the air from in my lungs and I just let myself fall. As I'm falling I can hear Green Day's Boulevard of Broken Dreams playing on my internal radio.

"Noooooo," I hear the scream despite the whooshing sound of the wind flying past my ears, but I don't have a chance to let it register or discover whose voice it is. Closing my eyes, peace finally fills my body before darkness takes over.

Ryker

Frantically speeding down the old railroad tracks on my bike was as difficult as it sounds, but I knew that I could get down the track faster on my bike than on foot. The panic gripping my body is all encompassing. I didn't know which way to look, which way to turn, or even which way was up by this point. All I know is the knot forming in my core is telling me to head this way.

The headlight on my bike is shining a steady beam of light ahead of me, giving me enough time to move out of the way of the different obstacles. It wasn't a wide track, just big enough for me to fit down without having branches smacking me in the face and chest. At the speed I was doing, if there where any branches it sure as fuck would leave a scar. However, losing Isabella would leave a bigger scar. She's the only person I've ever truly found a connection with since my father's death or maybe even before. It's a connection that means everything to me. I hadn't understood how dark and bleek my life had become until she shone her light and goodness into it.

Going back to that day in the courtroom waiting area, when she graced us with her wicked humor, a spark was awoken again. I didn't want to admit it at the time, but colours had come back instantly and everything was in surround sound. Any memory before that was black and white, but after her everything is a rainbow of colour. I may have lost my dad, but I wasn't losing her. Fate herself wasn't going to keep me away from her. I will fight for her tooth and nail.

By the time my headlights caught her, what I saw stopped the air dead in my lungs and brought my bike to a sliding stop. Before my brain could even register what was going on, I could feel my mouth opening and a scream coming out. But I wasn't fast enough. She just let herself go. I pumped my legs as fast as they would go, but I knew I wasn't going to be fast enough. Without a second thought, I launched myself over the side of the bridge to follow her down.

Hitting the cold, dark water is robbing me from all my senses. The song Red Cold River by Breaking Benjamin unabidingly pops in my head at such an inappropriate time. Kicking my powerful legs as hard as possible, I make it to the surface and inhale a deep breath of air. While treading water and spinning in circles I realise I can't see her anywhere. The current is strong and has already started taking me down the river, despite the fact it looks so still from above.

"ISABELLA!" I bellow while twisting my head in every direction. The need to find her burns through my veins. Lucky for me, I used to be on the swim team. Pumping my arms and legs to force myself through the water and with the help of the fast moving current, I'm able to cover a lot of distance. Just as I can feel the panic start to settle in again, I catch a glimpse of bright pink in the green shrubbery running alongside the river.

By the time I reach her, she is deathly pale with blue tinged lips. "Come on baby, come back to me," I whisper, while moving her damp limp hair off her face. Keeping one arm around her chest, I use the other to grab a hanging tree branch. Trying to heave us both out of the rapid water proves to be difficult. My shoes keep sliding off the wet grass and not giving me enough traction. Giving it one last powerful heave, I manage to drag our sopping wet bodies out of the water.

Moving my head down to her mouth, I can't feel any breath against my cheek. I mentally remember what I was taught in first aid and tell myself to start compressions on her chest to a count of thirty and then breathe air into her lungs with two quick breaths. "HELP!" I manage to scream out before starting the compressions on her chest. "SOMEONE, PLEASE HELP ME!" I plead into the dark night, making myself hoarse. After three sets of compression my arms start to shake with fatigue, and dread starts to settle in. I can feel my energy draining. "Baby please, I need you. I can't lose you, I've only just found you. Please come back to me," I beg, sobs wracking my body. I don't even remember feeling this desolate after my father committed suicide. I should have known Isabella was going to do something like this, I could see her on the same downward spiral; the booze, the sex, the partying, but most of all the constant look of pain in her eyes when she thinks no one is looking. Little did she know, I was always looking.

I begin sobbing into her chest when my arms give out and I can't push any longer. I don't hear the stomping of several pairs of feet through the bushes until they are right upon us.

"They are here"
"Found them"
"Get the ambulance prepped"

Loud voices are shouting different commands

around me. When a man in a hi-vis jacket and green overalls comes into the cleaning we are in, all my senses are on hyper alert. The flashlights are shining directly into my eyes, questions are being fired at me from every angle. But I just keep my body draped over hers, keeping her protected. Rough hands grasp my shoulders, painfully forcing me away from her, I kick out trying to fight back. The need to protect her is like lava burning through my veins.

Before I can blink, Zoe is in my face shouting, "THEY NEED TO HELP HER, RYKER! THEY ARE HERE TO SAVE HER!" Her words seem to bring me back to my senses. Realizing they are here to help, I move away and then crash. The adrenaline that had been keeping me going seems to evaporate in that instant. Standing at the side, shivering in my wet clothes, watching as the paramedics cut open her dress and stick orange rubber patches, with wires coming out of them, onto her chest.

"Charge to 200."
"Charging."
"Ready? Stand clear."

I watch as Isabella's body arches off the dirt encrusted ground and lands back down with a crack.

"No rhythm."
"Charging to 300."
"Stand Clear."

Again her body comes off the ground and back down again. It's ironic really, that my heart is beating a mile a minute, beating so hard it feels like it is going to beat right out of my chest, while hers has no beat at all. If I could give her mine, I would.

"Let's try one more time before we call it."
"Charge to 300."
"Stand Clear."

Everyone stands back with bated breaths, looking for any sign, any movement, anything to show there is life there. "Come on baby, come back to us, come back to me," I rasp out as her body curves off the ground again. It's quiet and slow, but I have never been so happy to hear a tiny beep in all my life and then there's another. After the second beep everyone seems to jump into action, almost as though they were convinced the final try would not work.

"She's in sinus rhythm but it's brady."
"Lets get her to the hospital before she crashes again."

They strap a neck brace on and secure her to a hard orange gurney to carry her out of the wildlife. I collapse down onto my knees and cradle my head in my shaking hands. The now wet ground where her body had been laying has a large pool of blood left behind. The sight of that will forever be branded into my brain and I'm left wondering where it came from.

Chapter Twenty Five

Isabella

I slowly blink my eyes open several times to try and remove the grogginess I'm feeling. Glancing around I find myself in a bright, unfamiliar room. It's a hospital room with pictures of beaches on the wall and comfy looking furniture. I'm lying in a bed hooked up to several different types of systems, all bleeping a steady rhythm. I'm covered with a hospital gown and blanket, but can still see the wires extending from my body. Several people are sitting around the bed staring at nothing in particular. Nothing is being said by anyone. They all just seem lost in their own thoughts. The T.V. is playing on the wall, but the sound is down low. Once again I can feel myself being pulled back into darkness.

When I come back into the bright room again, there seems to be some commotion. The same people as before are there, but a heated argument seems to be the root of the disturbance. Two men are shouting and pointing fingers at each other. The girl tries to get in between them to stop it, but one of the guys just picks her up and moves her to the side. Then the guys seem to go at it again. I wish I knew what they were fighting about, but it all just sounds like a buzzing noise in my ears. Glancing over at the window, I can see the lights outside shining brightly. In the reflection I see a nurse enter the room capturing the guys attention and causing them to stop arguing. As before, everyone goes back to their spots around the room and darkness settles in again.

I find myself again in the too bright room. This time it's different, there is only one person here. He's sitting in a chair with his body leaning over onto the bed. One arm is laying flat with his head resting on it and the other is on my lap grasping my hand. His shoulders seem to be moving up and down as if he is sobbing. Glancing over towards his face, I can see the steady stream of water leaking out of his puffy red eyes. I have this driving need to run my hand down his back, to tell him everything will be ok, to stop his crying. But I can't. I'm stuck in this limbo, in this nothingness place that feels weightless and numbing. I don't feel happy or sad, I just feel empty. His crying seems to finally come to an end, and he starts talking to me. I can see his lips moving, but I can't hear anything, except the beeping of machines. It feels like I should have this urgent desire to know what he is saying, but I just can't seem to find the emotion to care. Whatever it is that's he is saying, it's the same few words repeated over and over again. His head turns to look behind him as the girl from before comes walking in holding two cups of what looks like coffee. She passes him one while rubbing her hand up and down his back. Suddenly, I'm blinded by pure rage watching her ability to comfort him and being reminded of the fact that I can't. Before I'm able to do anything, everything goes back to darkness. But this time, I'm dragged back kicking and screaming.

I feel myself coming around, my body feeling heavy, my head pounding. Each of my limbs feel like a dead weight. I try to move my arm over my eyes to cover them from the blinding light, but it just doesn't want to move. Jesus, last night must have been one hella night to have this bad of a hangover.

"Isabella, can you open your eyes?" I hear an unrecognisable, but sweet voice ask. Oh God, my mouth is stuck together. I need water, I'm so parched.

Trying to use my voice, only a tiny squeak comes out. The atmosphere in the room changes, I can hear several pairs of feet rushing around all talking at once, making the pounding in my head intensify.

"Everyone stop!" the sweet, but stern voice demands. "Isabella, you're in the hospital. We need you to open your eyes, you had a bad accident." What the actual fuck? Forcing my body into action, I open my eyes and lift my arm to shield the light. When my hand is in direct line of sight, I can see several weird wires and tubes connected to my fingers and in my hand.

"What happened?" I croak out.

Grabbing a small cup with a bendy straw, Remi is the first to reach me. Leaning down he grips my head, holding the straw to my mouth. "Slowly Issy, small sips. You have been out for a while, we will have to get your stomach used to liquids and foods again," my best friend says.

"That's right," the sweet sounding voice comes again, "You have a very smart friend here." Glancing over, I see a petite woman in light blue scrubs, her top depicting cartoon bears. Unfortunately, turning my head has caused the throbbing in it to start up again. Gripping my head to try and stop the pain doesn't seem to achieve anything. The pain is still there, sounding like a whole African tribe are beating their drums on my brain.

"Is your head hurting, dear? Want me to get you some pain medication to help? A doctor will be along shortly to check you over. You have been out quite a while, you gave them all quite a scare," she responds while checking over the IV connected to the back of my hand and nodding towards the people around me. Looking around the room, my eyes catch on him, standing over by the window like a statue. When our eyes meet it's like an electric bolt is shot through my body. I can feel tears pool in my eyes and one blink is all it takes for them to break free and run down my face.

Ryker is by my side and grabbing my hand instantly. "Shhhhh baby, don't cry, you're ok," he whispers while giving my temple a kiss. Having his lips rest against my skin feels like home. I want to get out of bed, and climb into his arms and have him hold me. He must see the thoughts flash across my face. He drops down to sit on the bed, wraps his arm around my back so that his side is leaning against mine. I rest my head on his chest and while I'm gazing up into his eyes, a light tap sounds on the door and an older gentleman with a white coat and stethoscope around his neck strolls in.

The new doctor and the nice nurse exchange a look, "Uh, Miss Jonson, he really can't be on the bed with you." Before I can open my mouth with a snarky retort, Remi is there telling them to just let it go and move on.

"Okay, well then, hello Isabella. It's nice to finally meet you. My name is Doctor Barbodo, I'm one of the specialists on your team. I have been focusing on your neurological activity, along with your nerves and spinal cord," he says this while collecting the metal clipboard at the foot of my bed and flipping it open. "Do you have any pain anywhere, or any numbness or tingling?"

Clearing my throat, as it's still dry and itchy, I reply. "Um, my head hurts. It's like a bad hangover, must have partied too hard last night." I say with a chuckle, but no one else finds it funny. The tension in the room has been slowly increasing since the doctor arrived. Now it seems to have skyrocketed and everyone seems to be looking anywhere but at me. I can feel some big bomb is going to be dropped on me soon, I just wish I knew what the fuck was going on.

"Can you tell me, what is the last thing you remember?" The doctor asks while shining a light into my eyes. Guessing to make sure I don't have a concussion.

"I was at a house party," I glanced at Ryker, his eyes are bright and clear. Looking over towards Remi, he looks about ready to kill someone, his eyes have gone all dark and stormy. "Ryker said he had to go and deal with something." I didn't want to get him in trouble, if Remi finds out what happened, there will be a war. "I went looking for a drink as I was really thirsty and some strange guy started asking if I was a hooker and groped me." I hear a growl right next to my ear and Ryker's body has become like stone. Glancing up to see what's got him so mad, I watch a look of confusion pass between him and Remi. "After that, I ran off out of the house and down an old railway track." I can feel my eyes go wild when the memories come flooding back to me. Me sitting on the edge of the bridge with my legs hanging over, me standing up with my arms spread, me falling back. Oh God, I raise my hands up to cover my eyes and face. Oh fuck, I tried to kill myself. That was a huge fall and the river was fast moving, how the fuck did I survive?

"Anything else after that?" he says looking directly at me, as if he can see straight through my skull and directly into my brain. I don't want to admit what I tried to do. Everyone will just think I did it to be selfish or to get attention. But in fact it was the complete opposite of those reasons.

"No sorry, it's just blank after that," I say quietly, the shame of what I'd done still hitting me hard.

"Well, you have been in a coma for three months, so memory loss is normal," the doctor informs me, in a matter of fact voice. "I'm sure it will come back to you in time."

"Excuse me," I squeak out. "Did you just say three

months? I was in a coma for three months?" My voice has gone shrill. The shock of this news has me shaking. I look over to Remi, searching for the truth on his face, but it's just blank. Moving my eyes over to Ryker, he seems to find a bit of lint on his trousers fascinating with the way he is staring at it. Suddenly I'm feeling really tired again, I don't think my brain can take this type of shock. "Um, I'm actually feeling very tired." I say, voicing my thoughts. "Can we talk more later?"

"Yes, of course you are. Let's give you some space so you can get some more rest, but we will have to run several tests to find out the extent of damage your brain sustained after the fall and to see what, if any, kind of muscle shrinkage we could be dealing with. Surprisingly though, your spine had no injuries. You have got a long road of recovery ahead of you, but I'm sure you will make it," he says with a fast exit out of the room. I'm not really paying attention to anything he has said since the words three months and they now seem to be repeating themselves in my brain.

Chapter Twenty Six

Ryker

I sabella lived three months in the blink of an eye, whereas, it has been the longest three months of my life. My time has been spent between the flat, looking after my sisters, and in this hospital room. Zoe has been helping me loads with taking care of my sisters, as I get very antsy when I'm not at the hospital. I come and just sit and talk to her, tell her what my sisters are up to, read her favorite books or just hold her hand. The doctors didn't know when she would be coming out of the coma, and I didn't want her waking up and being all alone. I'm adamant loneliness was one of the factors that led to her jumping off the bridge.

After she had been brought in, the doctors had run every test possible. They had originally told us that the section of the brain she had damaged on impact was part of her visual cortex, which could lead to several complications; one being blindness or even the ability to recognize faces. So everyday, I would come to the hospital and the first thing I would do is take her hand and run it over my face, describing what she was feeling. The thought of her not recognizing me was the equivalent to taking a thousand blunt knives and stabbing them repeatedly though my heart. The fear of her waking up and not knowing who I was, sat as a heavy weight in the back of my mind.

When she had finally opened her eyes and looked directly at me, my heart had stopped beating in my chest for those few seconds. Our eyes had locked and my stomach had dropped out onto the floor below my feet, but as soon as I saw the recognition cloud her eyes, it started beating double time. A fire started from my heart and like lava, spread along through my veins, until it felt as if I was going to combust on the spot. I had promised myself that if she didn't recognize me, I would spend all my time having her get to know me again.

I had even brought my sisters to the hospital to meet her. I had explained to them that she was like Rapunzel. She had lived in a big tower all by herself. She'd wanted to leave, but her hair wasn't long enough and she had ended up falling out of the tower. They had read a story to her and helped me paint her nails and brush her hair. I wanted them to know where I was spending all my time when I wasn't with them. They had told me she looked like a princess, but more like Sleeping Beauty as Issy looked fast asleep. I couldn't bring myself to explain to them what a coma was. Plus, they had experience with our own mother sleeping all the time.

The bitch hasn't changed any in the last three months, except she has been on my case more. Apparently the flea infested shithole was looking more messy. Spending all my time at the hospital looking after Isabella meant it wasn't up to my normal standards. But still she doesn't care enough to pick up a mop or even a vacuum cleaner. Zoe has also been helping me in that department, making sure I kept on top of the washing and having food in the house. More to the point, I started to notice that wherever Zoe was, Remi seemed to be. Something has grown between them over the last few months. I have seen it in the small touches and looks that they have been giving each other. They would whisper into each other's ears when they thought no-one was looking.

So his pompous ass got to see the inside of my place, along with meeting my sisters. As if that wasn't bad enough, my mother decided to offer her services to him. I could only laugh and walk away, leaving him to fend for himself. I also had the pleasure of meeting Remi's parents, they had come by a few times to see Isabella. Her own parents however, have still yet to be seen.

It breaks my heart that her own parents hadn't bothered to visit her in hospital. She had tried to kill herself for fucks sake and nothing. To be honest, I think if they had come I would've had a few choice unwelcomed words for them. That most likely would have ended with me being escorted from the hospital by a few men in uniform and my wrists cuffed.

I have also been back to our beach a few times since the incident. Mostly to watch the sun set, needing to clear my mind from all the rage I have been feeling. I knew that place would quiet the angry voices in my mind. It had dawned on me, there, at our special place, that maybe fate had brought us two together for a reason. I was meant to save her, like she had saved me.

What had been the most shocking of all was her room. For someone who has over a million followers on Twitter and is one of the highest searches on Google, her hospital room is pretty bare of any cards or flowers. After the news broke about what had happened, the police had been called into the hospital to stop the paparazzi from getting pictures, but no one cared about her personally. They had just wanted the next top story. After a few weeks, when there had been no change in her condition, the news outlets had moved on from her, onto the next grizzley story.

When the doctor has left the room, following his bombshell that she has been in a coma for three months, Isabella looks visibly more deflated, if that's even possible. She curled up into a tight ball, and fell fast asleep. Remi had followed the doctor outside to finish up on all the plans he was putting in place for when she leaves the hospital.

When Issy had been brought in and her parents went MIA, Remi had stepped up. As much as it had killed me to hand the rights over to him, I knew nothing about her medical history. When they had started asking me about allergies and medical conditions, I had nothing to give. But thankfully Remi managed to get Power Of Attorney and being her best friend, had given them all her details. When staff had told us the outcomes, he made sure she had all the top doctors working on her case. He's actually a pretty decent guy, he stepped up when there was no-one else around to do it. Don't get me wrong, he still has a face I want to punch, just not as often or as hard.

"You ok?" Zoe says from the window seat. That has been her spot whenever she is in the room. Her past makes it hard for her to be in hospitals and I love her more for putting that to the side to be here for Isabella and me. They had become close friends while doing community service together. They may be from different worlds, but I've seen a true friendship blossom between them. I hope that doesn't change.

Glancing down at Isabella, I watch her eyelids flutter from whatever images she is dreaming of. "Yeah I'm good," I respond with a small smile reaching my lips. My heart wants to soar at her waking up, but the future is still so unknown. I need to explain what she saw between me and Conor, I need her to understand. Good God, I need her to understand more than anything. Remi has offered us a place, somewhere to move myself and my sisters into, away from Dave and his threats, but my mother won't let me take them anywhere. If I take them she will lose her state benefits for them. So that is all they are to her, a money bag. Now, Dave is a whole different story.

"It's such a relief to have her wake up, but I think it's going to be a long road to recovery," Zoes says tinged with sadness, her mind seems to be elsewhere as she watches out of the window. The hospital is a private one, overlooking the south bank of the Thames. At night you can see the whole city, with its twiling lights. "The doctor told Remi that he wants to move Isabella to The Wellington Hospital as it has the best rehabilitation center for neurological accidents. Doctors prefer to do treatment at home, but with Issy on sucide watch, they can't send her home without her parents being there." Listening to Zoe talk about Isabella like she isn't sitting in the room with us, makes me want to fly off the handle.

"Now that she has woken up, why don't we ask her what she wants to do? I'm sure she is sick to fucking hell and back of everyone else making decisions for her. In fact, I'm sure that's the root cause of the reason she is here," I snap back at Zoe, watching as her body visibly flinches from the verbal attack.

"Yeah, guess you're right," she mumbles to herself, looking as if her thoughts are miles away.

Chapter Twenty Seven

Isabella

When I come around again, the room is considerably darker. The pounding in my head has dulled a bit from the last time I was awake. After dozing for a bit, I decide I need to get out of this bed, a shower would feel damn nice. Raising my hand to rub sleep from my eyes, I notice a heavier one resting on top of mine. Opening my eyes, I see that Ryker has fallen asleep with his head and arms against my bed again. He looks like a fallen angel.

The moon causes a glow to fall across his face.

Even in sleep he has a deep frown line between his eyebrows. Using my thumb, I run it over the line trying to smooth the skin out and hopefully smooth out his stress. A deep moan rumbles out of his chest, and piercing grey eyes jump to mine.

His eyes run over my face taking every inch of it in, while I give his face the same perusal. I want to cry at all the small differences I can see there, from the new lines around his eyes, to the new gray hair around his hairline. I go to open my mouth to say something, but slam it shut again. What can I say to him? Where do I even start? The embarrassment I feel for what I have done to this guy forces my eyes away from his face.

"Look at me, please," he pleads in a quiet whisper. The desperation in his voice causes my eyes to fly back to his. "I have spent these past three months staring at your eyelids, wondering if I would ever see your eyes again." When he sees that I'm returning his gaze, he continues. "There are those beautiful green eyes that have been plaguing my dreams." He releases a sigh, as if he has been holding his breath this whole time.

"I'm... I'm." My throat closes up and I can't seem to get the words out that I need to say to this beautiful man. Screwing my eyes shut, he has been through enough pain because of me, he doesn't need anymore. I should be sending him away, making sure he doesn't come back. I would rip my own heart out just so he doesn't have to feel anymore of my pain. This beautiful soul deserves so much more than all the darkness my life is going to cause him.

"You should leave," I manage to spit out before my heart can stop my tongue from moving. I can't look at him. The pain, his pain, I know will stop me in my tracks and make me chicken out.

"No," he responds, firm and demanding. "I have to tell you, you need to know what you saw that night," he pleads with his palms up towards me. "I-"

"What?" I say confuddled. I just gave him the perfect out. I glance at him out of the corner of my eye. He seems relaxed, like he has no plans of going anywhere. "I'm asking you to leave." I start off quiet. "Just go. Your job is done, you have proven what a hero you can be. I don't need you to stay out of pity or whatever other complex you have going on. It's better for both of us if you leave, NOW!" By the end of my rant I'm full on yelling at him. Guess this is just like ripping a plaster off; you start off slow, until you realise it hurts more than if you did just one quick pull.

I watch as he raises up to his feet reaching his full height. Damn, I forgot how tall and broad he is. My heart just stops in my chest. He is listening to me, he is going to leave. The realisation of this hurts more than I thought it was going to. I look down at my hands, which are grasping the sheet on the bed. If I don't hold onto something, I think my hands will try and reach out to grab him. My body is full of dichotomy.

"Isabella, damn it, look at me." My body responds to his command before my brain has even registered his words. "I only work for Dave to protect my sisters. He offered his protection from all the gangs and all the drugs on the estate in exchange for a favour. Little did I know at the time that it would cause me to become part of his gang. After I had finished the one favour for him, he said as long as I carried on working for him, my family would be safe from the streets. I couldn't have my sisters ending up like my worthless mother, so I carried on with Dave's 'favors'. Everything I have done and continue to do, is for my sisters. The parking ticket that landed me in court was from parking in an ambulance bay at the ER, or rather A&E as you call it here, to rush my sister in when she was having an asthma attack. But without that ticket," he sighs "I would have never met you."

He ends with a pleading look in his eyes for me to believe him. I can only sit there and stare at him. Glancing down at the bed, I feel terrible for taking him away from his sisters. I'm so selfish to think that he had no one else to care for.

"You really should leave, you don't need my darkness tainting your sisters, they need you. I'm a big girl. I can take care of myself, but your sisters, they need a role model, someone to instill values and morals. I mean, who else can raise them to be badass females in this male driven society but you with your God complex." I look back up at him with a watery grin and a shrug of my shoulders.

"I am not now, nor will I ever leave you. You have my heart and soul. I will be spending the rest of my life showing you just how beautiful and amazing you are. Your brain," he says lightly kissing my forehead, "your body," he says kissing my temple, "your soul," he says finally bringing his lips to cover mine. "All of you, it has me captured and entrapped. Your light has been shining for so long but it has become heavy, let me help you hold it up. When your light dims I want to be the one to make it shine again. Just as you have done for me." This time he places his lips against mine in a more passionate kiss. He doesn't hold back one bit. His hands are around my face, tilting it back so he can plunge his tongue in further. It's like the man is trying to worship me with just his tongue alone.

He climbs on the bed and sits behind me with his arms wrapped around me. We sit like that till the sun comes up. I finally feel protected with him at my back, and surrounded by his love. I get this sense of calm and confidence that no matter what the world sends at me, I can take it on. With him, I can take it all on.

Glancing behind me, I raise my hand up to touch his face. It has more stubble on it than I remember, but the texture feels grounding. With a small smile on my face I finally say what I have been thinking since seeing this man in the court waiting room, "I love you."

Don't panic Ryker and Isabella's story isn't finished yet. Their story becomes more entwined with Remi and Zoe's story in Drawn to Danger.

Acknowledgements

I would like to thank everyone who has helped make this book a reality, Natasja without your organizing skill this book would be all over the place. You also help drag the ideas out of my brain.

Emma, my editor, you took the time to read over my story several times and reminded me it wasn't as shit as I thought it was.

My new tribe the 'Skanky Rebels' you girls keep me laughing like a loony in a crazy bin. I hope we have many adventures in our future together!

Gabbie Ash for making sure my head's on straight and pulling me out of the darkness when the light disappears. You have the hardest job of all.

To my Alpha reader Sam for her continued support at my crazy typos and terrible grammar. My beta readers, thank you for taking the time to read my shit and tell me when I'm wrong.

To you guys, my spanktastic readers. Without you guys my dreams of being a writer would never have come true. Thank you for taking a chance on me and for continuing to take that chance with every book I write.

About Kat Blak

Kat lives in West Wales with her two crazy kids, two adorable dogs and two party animal chinchillas. Yeah, she may have mild OCD with even numbers. Just don't fiddle with the radio or TV volume and you'll survive. By day Kat's a neurological scientist and by night a kickass author. Kat has loads of books floating around her crazy brain and they often come to her when her overactive brain is dreaming. So stay tuned as it's going to be a smut filled panty damping descent into hell.

Want to keep up to date on my new releases come stalk me here:

Facebook group: https://www.facebook.com/groups/TheBlakBirdCoven/

Facebook page: https://bit.ly/KatBlak1

Instagram: https://instagram.com/kat.blak

Amazon: https://bit.ly/KatBlak

Goodreads: https://www.goodreads.com/author/show/19787165.Kat_Blak

More by Kat Blak

Series

Silver Moon Duology
Book 1 - The Hidden Cure (https://books2read.com/u/3yE9QB)
Book 2 - Looking for the Cure (Coming 2020, co-write with Gabbie Ash)

Bad Girls Romance Series
Book 1 - Ride with Danger (Coming 2020)
Book 2 - Drawn to Danger (Coming 2020)
Book 3 - Escaping from Danger

The Crystal Collection Series
Book 1 - Within the Crystal (Coming 2020)

Daughter of Demons Trilogy
Book 1 - Infinity
Book 2 - Reveal Soon
Book 3 - Reveal Soon

Standalones

The Reaper Files (2020)
Hate Me (2020)
When the Dead Rise (2020)
Psychosis (2020)
Paranormal Halfway House (2020)

Playlist

Click here for the Playlist on Spotify

Def Leppard - Pour Some Sugar On Me

John Williams, London Symphony Orchestra - The Imperial March (Darth Vader's Theme)

Def Leppard - Love Bites - Remastered 2017

Cliff Richard - Devil Women

ACDC - Highway to Hell

Akon - Lock Up

Lily Allen - Fuck You

Hayley Steinfield - Love Myself

Kanye West, Jamie Foxx - Gold Digger

Riton, Oliver Heldens, Vula - Turn Me On (feat. Vula)

Divide The Day - Fuck Away the Pain

Kevin Lyttle - Turn Me On

Black Eyed Peas - My Humps

Green Day - Boulevard of Broken Dreams

Breaking Benjamin - Red Cold River

Printed in Poland
by Amazon Fulfillment
Poland Sp. z o.o., Wrocław

63716931R00132